THE RED
TRUCK

THE RED TRUCK

RUDY WILSON

ALFRED A. KNOPF NEW YORK 1987

THIS IS A BORZOI BOOK
PUBLISHED BY ALFRED A. KNOPF, INC.

Copyright © 1987 by Rudy Wilson
All rights reserved under International and Pan-American Copyright Conventions.
Published in the United States by Alfred A. Knopf, Inc., New York, and
simultaneously in Canada by Random House of Canada Limited, Toronto.
Distributed by Random House, Inc., New York.

Library of Congress Cataloging-in-Publication Data
Wilson, Rudy.
The red truck.
I. Title.
PS3573.I468R4   1987   813'.54   86-46128
ISBN 0-394-55846-4

Manufactured in the United States of America
First Edition

FOR MY BROTHER DAVE

I am indebted to the Copernicus Society and to James Michener for assistance, to Jack Leggett for encouragement, and to Gordon Lish for his guidance and his vision of my work. R. W.

THE RED TRUCK

THE ICEBOX

Ned was dead a year; his bed was cold and silent. Mama K died after he did. She was my grandmother. Her face always reminded me of corn. She lived in the pink room. My parents were far away in the new room, at the back of the house. We were all there, by ourselves, with everybody else in the world.

We lived on a hill above the dirt road that led to the orphanage. They had the steel push merry-go-round. I thought of it, so still and shiny in the night. The wind blew on it.

I had only one friend, a little girl, I knew only in dreams. I was with her almost every night. I dreamt of her even before she was born. She had yellow hair, short, and jagged, always messy, with her hands always at it, and up to her face. Her face—it was never clear. It was small, and narrow; I knew I'd like it if I saw it.

I heard her outside walking across the red boards that covered the broken sidewalk. The hollow sound made me smile in my bed. I wanted to see her so bad. I tried to make circles in my mind, to get back to sleep, but I couldn't. I could never catch up with the beginning of it.

The night the little girl was born, three hundred miles

from my house, I had a bright, white light in my sleep. I saw her coming out. It woke me. I was drenched with it.

"She's born," I knew. "She's here," I thought. I looked out the window at the Southern night—it was the beginning. It, and everything else I saw, was never the same to me again.

Years later, I knew her as Teddianne.

The next day I killed Dusty, the neighbor's dog. I sang my name to the air, up to the blue, blue sky.

"Bill-y," I cried. "It's me, Bill-eee!"

I threw my head back, wishing I had more hair like she did. The colors were out against the blue, as the sun burned into my eyes. It was like her.

"Dusty! Hey, boy! Come on—Dus-tee! Here I come—out of the sky!"

I was on the rafters high up on the side of the Gordons' garage. The roof there I could reach up and touch. It was warm. It was green and had a tar feel, a leathery bend to it. It sparkled.

"Look out below!"

I let go of the board. It was smooth, and ran longways. It was a new one. It had lines in it like flesh. I felt a long time falling. I felt my hand still on the board. The past was stuck to me like things; I felt it stretched out behind me. I fell through the air. It ballooned up my pants; my hair was straight up. I was so alone.

The dog looked up at me. I had a down-turned scar on my face from him. It was still tender, pinkish. Two weeks before, I put my face down on the warm cement close to his. I felt his dog breath on my face. I breathed his breath in. I

4

reached out and petted him. We were down at the Masonic Home, the orphanage at the end of the street. None of the children were outside. Their home was a gray one, and always looked silent to me.

He bit me in the face. He scratched my neck. I ran home up the old dirt road packed with treasures Ned and I had dug for. It was pockmarked.

On the way home I missed Ned more than ever before. I cried in the bathroom with the door closed. I leaned against the mirror.

I didn't mean to kill him. I landed on him and his sides ripped out. I heard the sound it made. It surprised me. My legs lay in his blood. My backside hit hard on the dog's body. I smashed the life from him, mashed the yellow dog's face closed forever. He had split open too easily, like he was expecting it. All his colors came out. I felt sick like the way I felt when I rode the turning, spoiled wheel down at the Home.

I had to go to bed early because of the dog. I fell asleep fast, but then woke up, out of breath. I had been out of breath for a year. I thought, "Maybe she has scars on her face, too."

Ned died a year ago. We got inside an old icebox down by the creek near the little woods. Ned was six; he was small. The door closed with a metal click. We had Southern accents; we talked in the dark.

"There's no light in here," Ned said. "I want to get out now."

"We can't," I said. "We'll have to wait till they find us. Mom'll come soon. She'll find us."

We were in there for over an hour, whispering, quiet and close. We were naked inside our clothes, inside a white box, curled up. The thin rubber seal held the light and the air away from us.

We waited. Ned told me some of his animal dreams, his dreams about wings. He had pictures of wide-winged birds in crayon, in his room. He said, "I had wings once. A long time ago, before I was me, like I am now."

I listened without answering. I felt I had always been myself.

I was there in the white darkness. Then I felt a mark, two marks, even with each other on my chest and back. They flashed in the dark, like small colored lights. I put my fingertip over the place on my chest where I saw it. I touched there, and I knew it was from her.

I was seven and a half. I remember seeing the outside of the icebox while I was inside it. It looked so alone there in the huge green yard with our awareness hidden inside it. I remembered the oranges that were always on top of the icebox at our house, soft, round, and orange-smeared-looking in my mind. Ned cried against me. The tiny light spot on my chest lit up his face, to see him by, one more time.

He remembered our daddy when he got his finger cut off that day when it snowed. He was cutting kindling for a fire. It was rare that it snowed in Mississippi. He had to cut the wood thin. It was orangish-colored. The snow wouldn't usually last very long, only sometimes overnight. We cut out paper men and hung them in the heat just above the flames. We tortured them to talk about things.

"They'll be talking soon," I said to Ned.

We knew they didn't know. And when they didn't talk,
they burned. The little men curled up, black. They screamed
for their friends, and for their wives and children, and for
themselves. They never wanted to die.

Daddy missed and hit his index finger with the hatchet.
I saw him see it. I think at first it didn't hurt him. He saw
the bone all the way through and the finger muscles. Then
the blood pumped out. He grabbed it and held it to his chest.
He clamped his teeth down and drew his lips back. He looked
to Ned, who had seen. Ned's eyes were wide-open brown.
Daddy said, "Go get Mom. Hurry." The blood dripped on
the snow on the ground by his knees.

"He fell to his knees, Billy-Billy. He held his hand like
he didn't want to see it. His face got white. And sad. Mom
came and helped him. He cried. Daddy cried."

We rested on each other's shoulders as the air got used
up, I felt separate from my body. My head felt grainy. I
thought of her; I almost felt a hand in mine. Maybe it was
Ned's. When the air started to be breathed twice, and three
times, Ned passed out. My head felt like it could pop. I
closed my eyes. I saw faces, like they knew something about
me I didn't. Then I heard yelling and pushing forward. My
heart pounded. I felt that I looked like an old man. I felt
something darker than the darkness I was already in come
closer. I yelled to Ned, but he was gone.

"Don't die," I said to myself. I saw the green yard behind
our house so full of air. I opened my eyes as wide as I could.
"Don't die, Billy-Billy," I said.

When the icebox was open, Ned tumbled out dead. He
had a purple face from no air.

I was alive. I had bigger lungs.

I was in a tired, dreamy state for days afterward. My brain got heated up. I got caught in a nightmare:

The man walked down the road, looking at the sky, feeling good. He looked at his feet in his old shoes. He stepped one more step—and fell in a hole. He climbed out and ran down the road to a friend's house—but he fell in another hole. Then he got out and went down the road to where the fat people live—and he fell in another hole. The dream in one of those holes were men with beards and with blood on their faces. They were all dead. I was in there, too. Someone was on top of me and had their arms around me. I struggled but they squeezed harder. I had someone's long hair in my mouth. I screamed and no one could hear.

Then it changed: I went deeper into darkness, where there was no air, where there were no people. The sweat poured out of me, it was cold. Mama K said I cried out in my sleep. I woke up. I had been to the center of the earth.

"To the core," I said. "It's under the meadow, under the ground, and under that, deep down in the middle, it's smooth. It's made of iron. It was solid, but inside it, deep, is the oldest air in the world. I got to breathe it in, so I could live. That made me older than anyone alive."

My parents nodded at me. They shook their heads. "That's all right, Billy-Billy. That's okay. You slept awhile and had some dreams."

"They weren't dreams," I said. "It was real."

I looked up at them from my bed. The bed was high up off the floor. We had wooden floors with floor heaters in them, like flat grills where the heat came through. I fell and cut a hole in my leg once on one. The sunlight came through the window. There were white curtains, blowing a little behind my head. I turned and looked out the window at the green outside. It was good to be awake again.

My parents were standing and watching. Mama K sat in the corner of the room in her wicker chair. Her eyes would close from time to time for minutes at a time. Something was in my mind. It felt like a spoon. There was a shape in my head like that. I thought, "Like a spoon."

I felt my thumbs were as big as the room, easily filling it up, and then it was so tiny at the same time. My mouth felt fuzzy. I felt I had been here before. Not *here*, not with these people or in this house or as a boy lying in a big white bed, but had *been* before. Then I lost it, I forgot what it was, and I was me, Billy-Billy. I still felt the spoon, but now softer, like it was watching me from a great distance.

I looked at Mama K's closed eyelids, old closed eyelids.

Her in the wicker chair.

It was summertime.

I felt her arms resting on its hard lines.

"Where's Ned?" I asked.

"Bless his little heart," I heard Mama K say.

She was holding on to her chair with her spotted hands. She had white hair. It used to be red.

"Ned's gone, Billy-Billy," said my father. "We'll never see him again."

"Don't say that," said my mother.

"I remember," I said. "I know. But where is he now?"

"Honey," my mother said. She had Northern eyes. "Ned's buried, in the cemetery. At the Masonic Home, next to Aunt Stiva."

"In the ground?" I asked.

"Well, yes, he's in the ground. We had to put him in the ground. He's in something, though—in a coffin."

She looked to me like her whole face had been hit by a big screen, making tiny dents over it—like a big fly-swatter.

"We would have waited for you—but we didn't know. We had to go ahead." Mama K opened her eyes; I heard her whisper something to herself.

"He shouldn't be in the ground," I said. "How can he move or go anywhere like that?"

And I thought, "It was just like it was in the icebox." I saw it again, standing huge. It got mixed up in my mind with the gravestone that would be at his place. I imagined the neighborhood kids drawing on the icebox door. "Ned is Dead. Age six. He stopped breathing inside."

I remembered a day with my father and Ned and me, a day in the park where the white ducks walked in their green grass. We walked up near the merry-go-round. Ned and I had new crewcuts and new sunglasses. The ducks were so white. They crawled with orange feet and the sky was blue. That morning we made a record for my mother in a studio. My dad held me up to the sun. He looked at me. The bright yellow was blocked by my new round head. He looked at my face. He held me.

His fingers were thick and he put me up on the wooden horse that had a painted face, and the hard, flowing, gray mane, and I rode. I looked for him at the curves. I had one hand free. I saw him through the darkened sunglasses that made everything look sharp and blue at the edge. He watched me. He stood there, strong, with his legs apart some. Ned was on another horse; now he was gone.

"You need to rest, son. You must need more rest," my

father said. "Mama K will stay with you. Me and your mom will be in our room if you need us."

I could see how he was just like me, hurting, with that cut-off finger, and his son out there in the ground. I didn't say anything to him. He said something to Mama K when he left that I couldn't hear, but I thought I heard the word "Jesus."

After Ned was gone, I was with Mama K. She read to me. She listened to me read aloud. She said it was good. She shook her head up and down. "You read good, honey. I love to hear your nice voice." Then she told me about Jesus some more and how He likes children.

I said, "How come I've never seen Him, or even felt Him close if He takes care of kids?"

I liked Jesus' name. He seemed tall, white. I pictured Him on the water in the wind. I tried to remember if He had been with us in the icebox.

"He's in your heart," Mama K said. "Deep inside, where it's quietest. It's a different kind of seeing. It's a presence. If you don't feel it, it's okay, because He's there anyway. He loves you no matter what you do."

"No matter what?" I said.

"He loves you no matter what," Mama K said. "He can't help Himself."

I thought of people and their souls, like outlines, filled with colored lights; like Christmas lights, blinking on and off.

I said, "Are you gonna die soon, Mama K?"

She said, "I don't know, Billy-Billy. I can't say. Why

don't we take a walk down to the Home and you can ride on the wheel—you can go round and round and round."

Mama K was looking at me. She was a large woman. I felt she saw me as very small, a little person with a little soul, a small piece of something, the only piece left for her on this world. Her teeth were big and square. They were like the painted boards on the new room where my mother and father slept, away from us.

Mama K held my hand, and we walked down the road to where the dirt began. The road was littered with old paper cups and junk. Ned and I used to dig up metal things from under the clay. I once heard Mama K laughing about us digging up the missing orphans from the dirt road and Mom had said it was awful and Daddy had that glassy look and was nodding his head; they were all holding cold drinks on the screened-in porch. Usually we just found old bolts and one time a little colored top that still spun.

The children that lived at the Home were almost never seen by me. But back behind the Home was the cemetery with the narrow paths going in between the graves. I knew that Ned was in one, under the ground, by himself. I thought it would be interesting if two people were ever buried together in one box, two people who really liked each other.

I wanted to move the wheel to just over his grave so it could turn around and churn him up, pull him back so he could ride and keep hold this time.

MAMA K

We had thunderstorms that smelled metal-gray in the summertime. I used to stand near the kitchen window at the double porcelain sinks and watch as the wind blew in my face. My mind carried with the wind, going to places in myself, and outside, around the town; and Mama K asked me, "Where do you go like that? Inside yourself?"

"Yes, ma'am, everywhere," I said.

I could smell things in the air coming at me from the distant horizon. I watched it, waiting, for something to appear. Mama K bought me toy cars to push on the rug. I listened to her popping gum at the ironing board. Its hot dry smell went up into my nose and warmed me. It went in like a thin line through me into my lungs.

Mama K held my face with the hands that shelled pecans. They were warm and old. She showed me how to make pot liquor out of cornbread, gravy, and field peas. She always said, "I vow." Her name was Kathleen. She was tender with me. She told me about the small town where she was born long ago. I followed her around the house and the yard. Daddy said we were too close, spent too much time together. But it didn't matter. Mama K loved me most. She used to say we were old, old friends.

She told my father how she felt about me. "You know," she'd say, "I feel I'm more than his old grandmother. It's different since Ned. I feel we're alike. We're friends. From a similar place somehow."

I saw Daddy look at her with a smile that went to one side of his face. He had a brown liver spot at his right temple. His eyes were soft and brown, too. Mom said he was too easy with me—and everything else.

"Yeah, Mama, you're a pair," he said. "I see how you are, together. Guess he'll be drinking home brew and rocking on the porch soon with you. I'm just going to let him be, to be himself, free for a while. It was a hard thing for him, the thing that happened."

My father rubbed his mouth as he spoke; Mama K must have always seen the missing finger on my father's hand.

Mama K was tall. Her son was about the same height and totally bald. They sat together often on the front porch. They had the look of the town on them, like Adolph Meyers, the fat man of the town who lived across the street, or like Ethel Gordon, with her frizzed beehive hair, one of the town's phone operators who lived next door. They all had an odd, almost mutated look.

Everyone knew Mama K and called her that. She had a white, sometimes yellowing look about her. It was her own father I reminded her of. Living with them all so close, I must have had a peculiar look about myself, too. In the mirror, my jaw looked a little crooked and my eyes were set in deep, sometimes so much so I wondered how I could see out of them.

"You ever been up North, Mama K?" I said.

"Sure I have, honey," she said.

There was something tall, white, way back in my memory, so faint, though, like an old taste forgotten. I thought about the icebox I had almost died in, as if the taste were left in there somehow, and sometimes I missed how black it had been.

"Did I ever tell you about my hometown, Electric Mills?" she said.

I said, "Can I lie down while you tell me? I want to think about some things while I listen."

I was almost nine years old then. Mama K wasn't that old, but it seemed like it to me. I watched her hands and listened to her scratchy, sometimes jumpy voice that comforted me. It was rain hitting on the roof when you're going to sleep at night. I looked up at her ceiling, of her room, at the marks up there. I saw them like clouds, imagining faces, and animals, some grinning, some mean. I saw moving herds of men up there.

"It was a very small town. It was a logging town, where the mills were. It was a small place to be in, not with a lot of people to bother you. We lived in an old brown house, square, but the kind that sort of stood up off the ground, almost like those river houses with stilts. It wasn't, though; it just had a different-color foundation on it. There were neighbors down the way."

"Like it had socks on?" I said, thinking about the house. "Like the black girls out at Woolworth's. They wear white socks with dresses, rolled."

She said, "You be careful downtown, Billy-Billy. Careful who you stand close to, who you talk to. You hear? Now, I

was starting to say I wore white socks with black shoes—
they came to my ankles. I can see myself running down the
road to my girl friend's house. Rosemary's. Her name was
Rosemary. She was a dear friend. I had red hair back then,
you know."

I saw it swinging when she ran as a girl.

"I met your grandfather there when I was sixteen. Married at eighteen."

When she said that, I thought of my friend Suzanne.
Her hair made her skin look white. I watched Suzanne's mouth
when she talked. She was in my grade, and had been paired
with me in the Easter pageant.

"Were there any stores in the town at all?" I said.

Lying on Mama K's bed made me remember a dream of
her from last night. I felt older, and with strange hunger in
it. I was laid out in a woods. I felt myself leaning on Mama
K's shoulder.

"We had stores," she said. "There was a drugstore down
at the end of our road, slap down to the end, past Rosemary's
house. Her father was a teacher. Quiet, quiet man. Killed
himself one day. Never said anything, just went and shot
himself."

I thought about the blood a gun might leave, and the
gun held close to the head.

"I wonder whatever happened to Rosemary. We left after
your daddy was born to come here to live. I was just a girl
then; I carried your father on my hip. Used to stroll in the
evenings; there were almost all dirt roads then. He was a
funny, quiet little boy. Always had his hair cut short. Looked
like he does now."

Now, she was with me as a little boy, and we snapped

beans into metal bowls that made the little sounds. I watched her when she made fried chicken. I licked the juices off the chicken with my fingers. I helped her outside, tending the flowers and the vines that grew on the trellis. Mama K reached tall, to the top. I painted the bricks on the house with my paintbrush from a bucket of water. It looked good, then it would dry, it would fade, and I'd have to paint it all over again. Mama K took the clothes off the line where they had been waving.

When Mama K died, the things in her pale room had a new line of silence around them. I felt smaller and colder in there. I lay on her bed and cried. The tears went into the white cotton bumps on her bedspread.

I sat up and watched my face get red and funny-looking in the mirror. The room was so still, and quiet, everything in its place but her. Mama K was up in the cemetery with Ned. I saw tears coming from my tiny-looking eyes that looked darker now. They were hot and my eyelashes got thick, and stuck together. Then there was a fist in my chest. It beat out at me. I squeezed my chest trying to get more air in, to smooth the cries I heard coming out. I gasped out; I moved up and down on Mama K's bed. My feet barely touched the floor. I bounced, I got light-headed. I bounced harder, and screamed, "Mama K! Mama K!" I bent my neck back and saw the big spots on the old pink ceiling. Now they scared me. They were so cold. They were killers. Then they were just dirty spread-out stains on an old dead woman's ceiling. I screamed and screamed. I bounced higher toward them and it was hard, very hard, to catch my breath.

THE MAPS

The flour and the salt hung in globs from my hands, stuck in between my fingers. I had red streaks on my face. It had taken me six months to make the maps. I had fifty salt maps in my room lined up against the four walls. I didn't have to go to school for a while—because of my situation. I flagged the major cities. Suzanne helped me. I liked seeing her squatting down in my room with the colors in her hands. She smiled a fox's face with colors streaked on her face like a mask.

Mrs. Royal was the third-grade teacher. She had shiny auburn hair tight to her old head; she had deep wrinkles on her round face. She lived very near the school on the corner. She drove a car with a big rear end on it. When I left school, she cried. My father pulled me out because of the breathing fits I had. I lay and waited for someone to come and get me from the ledge that surrounded the inner courtyard of the school. The playground was on the inside of the school. I lay on the cement and felt its roughness. I looked at the yellow-colored dirt we played on. It was my last day of school. I cried under the big tree at the playground's far end.

"I thought you were my friend," I told Suzanne. "I even thought you were her once. No one understands."

The kids laughed at me when I cried in class. Then I felt the black of the icebox and the darkness of the dreams; my past hung on my back and weighted me. I was intense and serious. I was as old as Mama K had been. I knew Suzanne didn't understand. Neither did I. She watched me cry and smiled at me when I left class to wait for my father to pick me up.

I stayed in my room now most of the time since Mama K died. I talked to myself. I made the maps. The room filled up with geography and color. I felt the heat and the cold and the wind blowing on my landscapes; the deserts, mountain passes, valleys, the moss on the trees hanging in the south, the beaches and the grains of sand, each one separate. My mind became like that—tiny, then large. I wanted to map the universe.

I stole a hatchet from the back neighbors and drove it into the wall above my bloody map of Maryland. My father made me take it back. My mother became small since the two deaths. Her features were thinner. Her life tightened up like it was tied with a wire that bit into her. Her mouth pulled into itself, a frown that was there all the time, like a scar. I saw the wire cutting off her head.

They talked about me, worried. I snuck up behind them late at night when they watched television. I sat in the wooden hallway with its TV shadows and heard the voices. Hers was thin and tight, his was soft and warmer.

"I'm afraid of him," she said.

I felt her voice like it was a ghost in the dark hallway.

"There's something distant about him, something in him that I don't know. He's too old."

"What? He's ten years old. But I know, though, I know. It's his imagination; it's taken a dark turn. He sees and he believes strange things. I don't know. Mama K could talk to him."

I felt her mouth being swallowed. "I'm not any good with him anymore. Maybe I never was. Maybe we should all see somebody. I'm just scared—nothing is the same. He's slipping away from everything."

I fell asleep in the hallway.

I awoke after them.

I was invisible to them now.

I dwelled on certain maps. I liked the salt map's porous texture to paint on, to create realistic grounds. I was drawn to Maryland in the geography books; I felt something there in my heart, it made my hands curl and tighten; so I set to work.

I made ten maps before I was through. I had the green, rolling hills, the gentle grounds of the land there, and the softer, light brown along the coastline. I put in the Antietam Creek and a flag for Sharpsburg, where the famous battle was fought. But there was something missing. I felt it, but couldn't quite picture anything. I got frustrated, mad; I bloodied up six or seven of the maps out of my anger, lashing them with the red paint, spoiling the calm green it had been. I left them alone on one side of the room, looking wild and torn apart.

I lay down in my tent bed with my hands straight at my sides, my hands up with the red and the green paint beginning to cake. I stayed there for a while starting to doze, feeling both colors seeping from my hands into myself, wanting to take hold and be dreamed about, with different feelings pulling at me, each tugging at one side of my mouth and causing a pull on my face. I could almost hear shouting in each ear, in the different sides of my head, when my father gave a loud knock at my door.

"Ho. Billy-Billy!" he said. "You in there?"

I was upset, and relieved. When I got up it felt like I left another, thinner, imprinted body in the tent, wrestling with the noise and the confusion. I opened my door. My room was like a different house from theirs, strange to have a visitor.

"Dad," I said.

I could see him looking at the maps.

"Why are you home today?" I said.

"I have the afternoon free. Are you okay? Were you sleeping?"

"I was resting. I made some more maps earlier."

I felt my teeth starting to grind in between words.

"You sure you like this room, Billy-Billy? There's no windows, there's no air. It's nice out today. You can always go back to your old room, you know."

"I know. I like it in here," I said.

He was looking at my Mississippi map. He avoided the Maryland area. "You got Jackson, and Meridian. Hey! Electric Mills. Who told you about that? Mama K? It was Gulfport where you cut your arm that time—remember? And Natchez. This is okay. This is a good map. We'll have to take a drive to some of these places this summer. Maybe we'll take a trip and go through Electric Mills. Boy, it's a long time since I've been there. You want to pass some outside now?" he said.

I was squeezing an orange I found on my table. I said, "Sure."

We went downstairs to the kitchen. I slid my hand down

the wide white banister where Ned and I used to slide down.
We kept the Christmas tree in the living room, where the
thick carpet was.

On Christmas morning, Ned and I had to stay in bed
until the light was strong enough to be able to see our daddy's
picture we had in a frame on our table at the opposite end
of the room from our beds. We had footlockers right at the
end of our beds and a small, brick-looking heater to dress
next to in the winter. It heated up and looked like the strange,
orangish lights on the walls downtown at the Temple Theatre.
The picture of him was from the air force. He had a sideways
smile on. He said he had no pants on in the picture, they
got him up so early, and that's why he was smiling funny.
They got them up early in the morning on the day they had
to go out and fight the war.

We went out in the backyard. I already felt weak; I
wanted to go back to my room. Mom watched us go out. She
watched from her back to us when we went by. I could see
the white straps beneath the white blouse she wore. Her hair
was near her shoulders, and I thought of her light blue eyes
hiding in slits.

"Here, catch!"

My dad threw me the ball. It felt big in my hands. I
threw it back. He walked about ten feet away from me. He
caught the ball with one hand. He had an old flat glove we
called the "1902 Mitt." He threw it back. I caught it, then
dropped it. It dribbled away and I scooped it up, tossed it
to him. The sun was getting very bright. It shone off my
father's head.

He rolled me a grounder. I had it. I flipped it back.

When I was born, he made up blue announcement cards

saying that a new center fielder was born. We passed a few more. He backed up some. The sun became insanely bright, and white, bearing down.

"Dad?" I said.

"Yeah!"

"Throw me a fly."

He did, and I caught it in both hands, but wobbly. He threw me another one, high in the air. I felt the wind blowing, and could feel the flowers swaying and the green light beaming out there in the yard, at me. The sky turned red with a powerful white, hissing ball in its middle. I never even put up my hands. The ball hit me in the face. It knocked me down.

I lay on the grass on my back. I felt years pass. My father rushed over. He knelt on the ground; he dropped his glove and lifted my head.

"What happened, Billy-Billy? I didn't mean it to hit you, son. Why didn't you try and catch it?"

My hands felt more separate. They lay in the grass.

"There was a bat last night, bucking against the window," I told him.

"What?"

"Last night, in the hall window, upstairs, next to Mama K's room, a bat. I saw his face."

He pulled me closer to himself out there in the backyard. I could see over his shoulder to the small woods behind the house.

"And someone smashed a wasp dead on the bathroom wall."

"Billy-Billy? Are you okay? Does it hurt? What are you saying?"

"I saw a person wearing a rat's face."

My father just looked at me.

"I just saw it coming, is all. I felt it hit me."

I could feel how big his shoulders were. He held me without moving. He had talked to the side of my head. He must have been looking now at the house or at the bright sky.

"I feel alone," I said.

I thought, "I don't feel young like I should. Not ever anymore like I used to."

"I don't ever feel good," I said. "I can't breathe good a lot, and I can't sleep at night. I wake up all the time."

I felt my mouth quivering into a forced frown, a strong thing inside me making me frown. I couldn't talk good.

"I'm scared," I said. There were pieces of pain all over my body.

I touched my nose, and it wasn't bleeding.

"It's all right," he said. "Don't worry about the nose. It looks okay."

He was looking at me now.

"That was a pretty strong blow you took, though. You took it pretty well," he said.

He held me, and he hugged me.

I felt our arms sticking out, our elbows. And him out there, kneeling down, and my legs sprawled out like a doll's. I saw a picture. I was in it. Thousands of people in a huge pile of arms and legs and bodies. I looked at my father's face. It was smooth, it had tiny black whiskers growing so evenly. He didn't know about what I wanted to ask him, about death, where people went, where they were now. So I told him a story. He watched my face when I talked. I was still crying some between some places.

"It's funny," I said, "but one time me and Ned were out in the yard and it started to rain. We could feel it coming, the sky got dark. We were sitting at the picnic table when the rain came, but it only rained in the front yard. It was funny. We saw it and we smelled it and felt the coolness of it, but it never rained in the back. We ran around to the front yard and it was raining hard. Ned was laughing, and we ran back around to the back here and it was dry. I guess it had to stop somewhere. We sat in the back and watched it rain. There was a place where it stopped, a clear line."

I saw Mom watching us from the kitchen window. I saw her with her hand by her mouth. She looked thin and wavy, like she wasn't really there. Dad didn't want to say much about the rain story.

"My face hurts. I want to go in and lie down," I said.

We walked to the house. When we got there, Mom was gone. Before we got to the house, he said I had to go to the doctor.

"About my face?" I said.

"About a few things," he said.

The colored maps flashed in my mind.

"Your mother can take you over this week. It will be okay," he said.

I went up to my room and listened to "Corina, Corina" on the radio. I could feel the singer's voice in my throat. It felt like I was waiting for things to come and happen to me.

THE POCKET

I had her in my pocket. I liked that she was in there, in that dark. Only I knew. I knew how we were the same. Her and me. And the link. The line that goes between us. It was a good day. The sun shone evenly, not too hot. The air was spring warm on my arm that stuck out the car window. I made the little man in my pocket—it was hard plastic—into a girl. Inside itself, it was a girl. On the outside it was what I had made it. I melted the head some and stuck an old piece of film on its head for hair, or a hat. Its eyes drooped from the melting. I carried it, and talked to Mom in the car.

We passed some woods. Mom seemed as small as me over on her side of the car seat. The woods had pine trees.

She asked if my chest hurt. She watched straight ahead, shifting her eyes to me for a moment. We stopped at a red light. The air was cool but sunny. The other cars on the street looked so clear, so clearly what they were. We were stopped, next to the woods. I thought about jumping out and running into them. I wondered how deep they were, if there were houses on the other side, or buildings. Could a person live in there without ever being seen?

"Yeah, it hurts some," I told her. "It always does."

I looked over at the side of her head. Her hair was black, and coarse. She had light blue eyes.

"If I take a deep breath, it catches, and I have to hold for a second, because I don't like to cough. Will I have to get a shot?"

"No, I don't think so. The doctor will just look at you. He'll listen to your chest. He might ask you some questions."

I turned back to the window. I thought that if I threw the little girl out of the car window, far into the woods, she would then get bigger, she would grow and get bigger than my mother, who is afraid to look at me, who talks to me from far away. The girl would be gigantic, her mouth would be red, and open, and she wouldn't talk. There wouldn't be anyone out there to talk to. I imagined her hands, strong, and holding things, gripping the whole woods, the trees, my hands. We drove on to the doctor.

"Maybe he'll give you some medicine, something to clear your lungs. Billy-Billy, do you think—of Ned when your breath gets caught, or at night when you can't sleep, or when you get nervous?"

"No."

I did, sometimes, but not like she thought, not in a way that was bad, or sad. He always stayed the same. I knew the doctor wouldn't find anything wrong. He'd look, and pretend to know, and if I told them about Ned, then they would nod their heads. I would think about the girl in the woods.

She said, "Oh."

She held the wheel with both hands. Her hair hung down in her eyes, over her forehead. She would hide her whole face if she could. My dad would push her hair back with his hand and look at her like her face was new to him. He'd say, "You're pretty with your hair back. You can see your face, Elizabeth. Why don't you ever wear it this way? Keep it out of your face, it looks better out of your face."

"It doesn't," she'd say, and she would shake it back down.

She was a Northern girl, had been. She wore men's corduroy pants in the winter, and blue jeans. In the summer, she wore shorts; she wore sleeveless blouses. I would see her wandering around in the backyard, under the tall thin pecan trees. There was something in her—quiet, secrets, that seemed to go with her being from the North. She was from another country. Her black hair and the lightness of her blue eyes made her sharp in contrast to the town, the heat. She drove into herself. Ned had been the baby; now I was, again.

"I hate that smell in the hallways of the doctors," I said.

"That's alcohol, and it's not at the doctor's. It's only at the hospital that it smells like that. Stop that," she said.

I was twisting up my face and rolling my eyes. People driving by could look through their windshields into our car through our windshield, through two glasses, and see me making faces.

"Stop it," she said. "Your face might stick like that."

Some people wore glasses probably that saw me in the car. That meant three layers of glass between us.

I said, "Don't you think it's interesting to think about things? Like to put your mind on a thing that's away from you. Then it becomes part of you, it's inside your mind then, at least for a while."

She said, "Where do you get ideas like that? You spend too much time alone. I want you to be out more, doing things

with other boys. I don't agree with your father about taking
you out of school. I don't think it's good for you. I think the
doctor can shed some light on this too for us. What happened
to Suzanne? Isn't she your friend anymore? I never see her."

"I don't know. But do you know what I mean, about the
things? Like see that fire hydrant over there? You passed it,
but when I had my eyes and my mind on it, it was more
alive."

I thought of her in my pocket.

My mother said, "We're here."

"Of course we are," I said.

"Don't talk like that," she said.

"Mom. Sometimes I miss you," I said. "Hey, I think
my breathing's better now, Mom. We don't have to go in.
Let's just take a walk. We can look around."

In the office was the smell. It was different from the
hospital one, but it was still the smell. The carpet made it
quiet. There was a little girl with a big man. He had a red,
ruined nose. His eyes were puffy and made tiny-looking. Their
color barely seeped out, looking black. He had his arm around
the little girl's shoulder. When I had watched them for a
moment, he shifted his hand under her thin white arm, and
then he held her hand in his. She was scared. Her eyes were
twice the size of the man's. Hers stared around, and black,
too. She had deep, dark lines under them, like trenches, and
her hair was thinned, like it was burned off. I could make
out the shape of her head. I looked down at the shape in my
pocket. The girl in the chair looked so slight. She might have
floated away if not for the bulk of the man. The man's hand
on hers was almost funny until I looked at their pairs of black
eyes.

I looked closer at her. She seemed weak, and lonely, like something thin, barely holding. She felt like Ned in the box. I looked at the big window behind me. A coolness lifted off from it on my back. I looked at my mother. She nodded, with her lips, thin, together. I put my face to the window. There wasn't enough air in the room. It was stale; it had smoke in it. The doctor probably smoked in it. It reminded me of a certain fish I had seen on a wrapper at home, a salmon, how its color was a cakey orange, stale in its canned death.

I put my lips to the glass. I felt the girl watching the back of my head. I turned to see her. She narrowed her eyes, and her mouth opened some. She kept looking. I saw her hand tighten on the man's. I looked back out the window. A man was cutting across the lawn, up a little incline toward some office buildings. He wore a dark suit with a tie that blew out of his coat. He moved quickly.

"What's going on out there?" asked my mother. "See anything?"

I thought, "There's a girl looking at me, wishing things were different. There's the big man, and there's me and you, and the girl in the woods, in my pocket, with a red mouth, that I've thought about my whole life, and then there's this man hurrying to somewhere." I didn't think it in words so much, but I thought it.

My mother had wanted a daughter, and to name her Aimee. She had been a daughter. Her father had left one day when she and her mother were in the city of Detroit, shopping. They were Yankees. When they came home, half the furniture was gone. She said there was no note. They had probably bought him a tie that day.

Ned had had her eyes. She sat in the backyard under the trees and cried after he died. He was her baby. She held on to the bark of the tree. I could see her back shaking, from the back kitchen window. They were pecan trees. The pecans had black marks, like the white marks on her fingernails, but black. I stood watching her at the window in my shoes that were white and high tops. I felt like standing on them to hide them, they were so bright.

I answered her. I said, "A man in a suit. He's walking in the mud, now. I can see the horizon between the buildings. You could walk all day and never get there."

I laid my head down on the back of the couch and rested. I reached for the horizon. Then I looked again.

The man was still out there. He was in the parking lot now, leaning against a car. He had one foot up and was scraping it with a stick. He kept doing it, back and forth, and wiping the stick clean on the grass.

"The man got his shoes muddy walking on the lawn," I said. I watched some more. My face slackened, my eyes relaxed. What he was doing brought sudden tears to my eyes. "It's perfect," I whispered. I had chills rush through my chest. "There's nothing else he could be doing." It was like a puzzle when the lines between pieces dissolved. I found the little, sick girl there—she was perfect, too. My mother sat in the seat next to me, her finger touching her lips. The big man was infinite.

Then I heard the nurse scratching with her pen. It made warm water run down my neck. She kept doing it, I hoped, forever.

"It's interesting out there," I said.

She said, "Uh-huh. That's good. We're almost next."

"Almost next," I thought. "Al-most next." If I said it again to myself, the words would have broken apart, and away, and I would have been left in between, in that place that's in between everything. I reached back for the girl again, and she was there in that same place. I laid my face back on the edge of the couch. My mother reached over and put a hand on my head, in my hair.

She said, "Are you feeling all right?"

"Yeah," I said to her. "I've got a hole in my lungs."

CHILD—
SPRING
1862

There was another boy, in another time, a different face, but still some resemblances. He looked like his father—the shape of his head and the eyes—the way they looked out. His father ran for the horizon, all day long. It was a warm day, in the spring, in 1862.

The boy felt something in his mouth, first in his teeth. They shook, with a slight vibration. His teeth were small. They looked soft, like white sweet corn that had pockets of juice in them, a child's teeth. They were harder than corn. The juice inside his mouth was young. He was twelve. He wouldn't live even one day more, or even one hour, but maybe he would live again.

The boy lived with his family; his father was gone to the war. He walked away in his wrinkled gray clothes, his long legs carried him farther and farther away, until he had become a dot, but there was still a walking rhythm in the watchers' eyes. And his long legs. His wife and two sons had watched.

The boy remembered that walking day now, in the most recent moment of his life. He sat on the planet that seemed big to him only because he was so small. He thought it must be smaller to his daddy—who had explained to him about the earth and the moon and the air held around it for them to breathe. Whatever it was that held the air in close enough to breathe wasn't even a distant concern, because he was about to stop breathing. His father was running to a battle, at a creek that was called Antietam. His breath was coming hard, and along with thousands of other men, he pulled and pushed the atmosphere around a small Maryland town.

The boy was Alan. He sat in the garden of the farm, touching the vegetables. The dirt was dry on his hands. His fingernails were long, dirty underneath. His younger brother, at ten, was tied by a long rope to a wooden pole thirty feet away. He chewed at it to get free. He had two teeth missing in front where they had fallen out. It was tough on the rope; his lips had a little caked blood on them from trying.

Alan held an eggplant in his hands. The skin of the vegetable was purple. It had a dull shine. He held his hands just over the plant, and closed his eyes. When he closed them, he barely saw his brother staring at him. When they were closed and dark, he imagined seeing Adele's arm rear back to throw a rock at his soft, closed eyelids or to tear into the thick-skinned purple. But he kept them closed. He lifted and brought his hand closer, seeing how far away he could still feel the life of the eggplant. He put his face against it. He looked from the ground level at the other vegetables he had grown.

He saw the lettuce heads. There was yellow squash. It was dull, with white on it. The gourds had the colors. Orange pumpkins, green cabbage, zucchinis, and the weeds that were thin brown, were sitting, waiting. The dirt, in its almost even rows, was about to be disturbed. Alan looked at the ribbed surface of the great, orange objects. They were like huge heads. He loved them. He grew them. He and his father put their hands down in one and pulled out the wet insides, ripping, to make a toothy face, on Halloween.

Adele at the pole ran in a circle. His blond, nubbed hair was streaked with dirt and sweat. He held his fingers to his face, pulling at his eyes, downward, making terrible faces. He had a toothy grin, too. His blue eyes with his hair—like straw and a blue sky. His brain was like a scarecrow's. Now he was tied to the leftover lean-to pole that had mostly fallen down. He had run away six times in six days, looking for his father.

The father built the lean-to, two years ago before the war started. Now he was a runner. He tried to make a tune or at least a rhythm out of his rattling gear and the gear of the other thousands. He was in the middle of the group, but it was more than a few times he looked for the group's edge, and farther for the solid horizon line. He wanted to go lie down in its dark line that ran and curved along with him. There were many, many who wanted that, some straggling and making points and vertical lines out there, and off into the woods. But mostly, their feet kept going on, pounding.

Irene was his wife. She sat in the dark house when the jarring started in Alan's teeth. It was a small, dark house— four walls holding against the space that pushed to get inside. Alan and Adele were born in the house their father made. And Allie, the little girl, too. Daniel was the father, who ran and who wrestled with the boys even in the mud, and came home one evening with them with a long barbed-wire gash across his back, hardly even noticing it, grinning, and beaming, a hand on each boy's head, one strong and thick, the other soft like straw. Irene felt the jarring in her breasts.

Irene made an invisible circle around the outskirts of their small farm. She walked it at night when their children were in bed. She could hear the swishing of her dress in the tall grass. She walked close to her neighbor's house. Sometimes, she squatted down and watched the other house, staring at it for long minutes. The war had changed everything.

One night, she came very close to the other, dark house, and listened at the half-opened wooden window. The neighbors were called Fitch. They had a colored bird in the house. He never sang when Irene saw him, and his eyes bagged down in circles. She liked his tiny tongue; she stared at it as it came out of his beak, like a tiny baby's. The man was crippled in one leg, had missed the war so far. But people feared the war would come to each home one way or another.

In the dark, she came close; she saw the butter churner at the corner of a wall; she looked at it almost in a personal way. Then she heard the Fitches in their bed. The colored bird was in her mind, probably under his night cover, she thought. "And I'm out here with the churner," she thought. She leaned her face against the rough wood wall and closed her eyes. She put her hand outside her dress between her legs and rubbed. She listened and then forgot to listen. She heard herself and Daniel. He whispered to her that she was beautiful. She held him with her arms and legs.

Daniel was from Tarlow, Maryland. He played the harmonica and met Irene at the fair when he was twenty-one. She was sixteen. She watched him playing the tinny music with his hands wrapped around the silver instrument. She liked how he looked, tall and skinny with long black hair that fell in his face in long pieces that he pushed back with his hand. He smiled at her with his eyes while he played. She liked that, and his narrow, easy-looking face and the feeling that grew between them.

She was the first girl he really knew. He liked the smooth wild feeling of her body. He kissed her with the mouth that played the music. They were married when she turned seventeen, on March 30, 1844. She remembered his hands that night by the Fitches' cabin.

She pushed against herself at the wall of the house. She looked up at the moon and the stars; there were no more sounds inside. A young child had wandered out into the yard. He watched her, then she saw him, and they both stared. She thought of her own boys at home, a mile away. She looked at the child's large-looking head. She remembered what it was like to have a head coming out of her, three times. She thought about pushing this boy's head up into herself.

"Stupid," she said to herself. "Evil." She thought, "The boys could be dead. It'd be me who killed them. Left them to die. I leave them to die every night." Then she knew, quieter, "I want a man, not this baby boy, to stick his big head in me. But something."

Irene rarely spoke to grown people since her husband left. She was left to think for herself. He had been gone for months. Her young boy ran away each day lately. She felt that was a sign of something bad. She thought about Daniel's blood, that he would die in the war. She imagined his blood covering the sky, red for days, like the locusts had done in some places. She pressed herself very hard inside herself until she wanted to scream. She said, with her eyes half-closed, "Come here, boy, and grab a stick," and she laughed out loud.

Before she heard or cared about hearing, a man's voice yelled out from inside, and she was off. She ran up the grassy hill. She swayed her body side to side in an extreme way as if the man were watching. She got about two hundred yards away; she began to spin with her arms in the air in circles.

"I wish I was dead," she said. "Just dead."

She pictured a fish in the dust, rotting, and a chicken with his head cut off.

"Fuck Robert E. Lee, and the rest of them."

She slapped her face.

"Yeah, I'd like to, I'd like that. I'd like that."

She felt heavy, and dirty, dragging herself home through the high weeds, the dirt in her shoes. When she got to the house, she came around to the front of the house, curved around its corner. "Daniel," she thought. "And the boys." She felt an urge to bow down below the loft where they slept. "Their blood is our blood, it's running through them." She half smiled, remembering the little boy back in the dark, and the thought of his big head. She looked up.

Adele wore a strap across him in his bed.

In the daytime, the boy ran along his worn path. He wore the grass down with his bare feet. He had ringworm in his body, the tiny holes in the bottom of his feet. He padded, but not hard enough to cause the jarring that his mother felt in her quivering breast. She touched it with her hand.

Alan forgot the vibration in his mouth. At first he thought about putting his ear to the ground, to listen, or a cheek to a railroad tie like his daddy told him about. But instead he touched the warmth of the purple plant. He had a small silver pistol in the waistband of his pants. He had his shirt out, covering it. His daddy had given him the small gun, and to his terrible surprise he hit a black cat at thirty feet, shot him twisting into the air with a sharp bang that lingered even now in the garden, in the bright spring light.

"Black and orange," he thought, of the cat, "alongside a pumpkin."

Alan followed his mother some nights when she made the big circle, and in the day looked at the smaller one his younger brother made, and thought about the one his father made when he came around home again. The sun went in a circle, too, and he looked at the roundness of the pumpkins. He put his hands to his head, feeling it to be very large. It felt hot. Things came up over the horizon from where you couldn't see them before, then they kept going until they disappeared. His hands went down to his waist. They felt the gun that he loved. "Things keep coming up over," he thought. His mind went out to the idea of the earth in its girth. "With a band of steel around it," he imagined, "and it spins." He looked down a straight furrow in the ground; he didn't notice any slight curve there. He could hear them coming now.

He turned around. He got up on one knee; he squinted his eyes and face just to see better who it was riding so fast at them from the emptiness. The dust rose behind them. Heat waves came on first. There were about fifteen men riding, wearing dark colors. He didn't know anything about them, but these were men who belonged only to themselves; they were part of no organized army. They had their own desires, their own circulating blood to take care of. They had been Rebels once, some of them, and the others just pure renegades. They didn't care, they just rode through the lives they met.

"Ma!" cried Alan. "Ma! Some men are coming!"

Alan felt shaky. His legs felt different, imbalanced. He felt like he was upside down. "Ma! Come look! They'll be here in a minute!" Alan cried.

Irene was in the dark house. She had heard the buzzing flies and the padding feet in Adele's rhythm. She cried the night before in her bed. She felt guilty; she felt bad about tying down her little boy. "But, hell," she thought. "I can't be running him down every day. And I am damn sure not going to do it at night."

She held herself.

There was a deep, almost agonizing pleasure in touching her body.

She lusted for herself. Her hands craved the touch. There came a guttural sound in her head that passed through her throat, rising up along the ribbed insides of her. It became high-pitched and her eyes half-closed. She closed her eyes and saw blurred lights, little lights softly at the low level of her inner sight.

She rolled her head.

In the day, she sat in the chair. Sometimes, the tears would seep from the corners of her eyes. Her hands felt her breasts like her son had touched the eggplant. She was in the chair when the boy yelled. She had been in a hazy state, thinking about nothing, just aware of her body and an ache in her mind somewhere distant. Her neck was curved back. Now she had a knot in her soft stomach. Her hands stopped there on it. She knew this was it, that she might be dead soon, or worse. She cared, but there was no choice. The whole country was dying, the dark spots spreading like blood on a cloth.

She stood up, suddenly aware of her hands.

She went to the doorway.

She hadn't bothered to button her shirt. It was Daniel's, coming down to her knees. The arms were cut off at the elbows. She saw Alan in the vegetable patch, his hands in front of him, held out in front of his chest. She saw his long fingers and delicate hands. "A shame," she thought. Adele made his way around the rotten pole, the rope rubbing on the old wood. She put her hand to her forehead, to shield the light, to see who it was coming. The warm air came through her shirt front onto her skin.

She jerked her head back. Where could she run? What about the boys? Alan was looking to his mother and back to the approaching men. She looked to the huge, spread-out oak tree. She'd have to make a run.

Dust rose from the advancing horses. She felt a man's hot, heavy breath on her neck, already. That woke her up. She heard a loud, "Caw, caw," above her head.

The caw sound lit the blue sky bluer. It swooped down to the woman's ear.

She remembered being a child:

Her own girl face. She saw its small oval shape, her hair cut to frame it at the chin.

"Caw," and the men got closer. One more scream of the bird, and she snapped.

She remembered: a child's foot in a new white shoe breaking a branch on the ground.

She ran. Her hand held her shirt closed, clenched together in a fist against her chest. Her other hand flew up

against the blue sky and the cawing that seemed to her to
come from all around her. The bird was in the narrow canal
inside her head. She understood inside, in layers, different
truths in each one.

"Layers and layers of light," she remembered from somewhere. Her body ran, she was scared. Inside it was slower.
"Layers and layers of light, each one making the other one
look like darkness." She was dying, she thought. Run.

The horses came onto the farm. Irene put one foot after
the other, remembering:

She sat on the little horsie; she lost her front teeth. An
old, one-eyed horsie. In 1831, she said, "Cakie. Gimme
cakie." She reached out a baby hand. She sat on the horsie
and ate the crumbling cake with the pretty icing that was
sugary. "Cakie," and a little wooden horse.

Her boys, one with the planet in his mind, the other tied to
a pole, helpless. Her foot fell, there—then, there. She watched
them fall. She looked up at the top of the tall oak. She wished
she was up there. She would jump rather than die at the
men's hands.

She looked back. She held her shirt. She could feel her
breasts underneath.

BLUE JAY

The shadow started at Alan's chin, and moved up. He looked older. He watched his own body from a short, wavy distance. His father, miles away, reached down to the side pocket of his flapping jacket. He held his watch in his palm. He took it out, opened it with his thumbnail. He saw it was 2:10 in the afternoon. He let the watch fall to the ground.

His watch tasted good to his children when they were babies. It was gold and had a shiny, metal taste to their tongues. It tasted like their daddy's hands. His fingers touched their eyes—and their mouths, their faces, turned to him. He washed them in a wooden tub. He licked the back of the baby that died. She tasted to him like Irene. On Daniel's watch, it said, "Love, Segrid, 5–23–15."

One man led the renegades. They flew through the homesteads. Frank Chaney was his name. He had had a life, a child, lost, and a woman, buried by the shade tree—dug up and burned, burned to forget. The dark blue dress crinkled and smoked as she caught fire. Frank Chaney rode with that smell and the sound of it burning, in his nose even now.

He reached down for his sword. It was just after 2 p.m., May 2. The sword reflected the day's light. The woman looked small to him, running like that. He pictured her blowing hair mirrored on the sword's edge, and her face that he couldn't see. He waved his sword. He saw the one boy, and the other small person, a child, but strange. The house was a smudge to his eyes as he rode by. He made a quick sweep of the vegetable garden. The horse stepped into the squash; the lettuce gave way. The pumpkins were silent.

Alan had his pistol. The green and the grass watched, the brown dirt clung to his fingers that shook. The wind that had blown his mother away, that blew her clothes away from her body, blew on him, and far away in his father's face.

As Irene ran she became a little girl. A laugh rose in her throat. She was aware of the farm animals nearby. The cats, she felt the cats' skinny bodies. She said, "Cakie." She squeezed the cat; he wouldn't eat the cake. He punctured her wrist with his teeth.

Running with Irene was another body; it ran in her chest, making small outlines, her braids flipping. Then a woman ran, lunging, working, pushing her legs, her mind floating to the top of the tree. She heard a harmonica over the sound of the cawing bird.

Alan pulled out his small gun. He looked straight into the second horseman's open mouth. He pointed there and squeezed the trigger. He blew a quarter-sized hole in the man's head. Wild, wild, raspberry-colored blood poured out the hole onto the man's back and onto his horse's back. A third man came on. He thought, "A boy! A goddamned boy!" His voice got into the furrows of the dirt.

Alan jumped. His shortness ran, his shadow crouched toward a tree that got two small bullet holes in it, one that came through the boy's head, coated red. The blood was on his neck, it dripped down there, past the sun-brown to the sun-missed whiteness of his body that pulsed and then stopped. He had tiny hairs on the nape of his neck and on his back. His mother ran her fingers there. He lay, now he curled up last into a circle on the ground. His lips touched the dust in the grass. In his throat was a lump of air connected by nothing to a point of being.

A long triangle started. It was Irene's and Frank's. The lines were drawn, one to her, one to him, and one to another man, who hadn't been figured on. "The gray and the blue," Alan thought in a vague way. He saw the red on his fingers, the red sun and the spinning of the flat earth dish on a long stick. That's what the boy, Alan, saw in his mind, his last thought.

Frank Chaney burned his wife, already dead. He speared her on a long pole, and held her, burning above his head. Little flames dripped down on his face and head. His face had wet, red-bright tears. He left his little girl in the ground. He stabbed at her grave with a pitchfork and a long spear, ending, trying to end it.

"Get away!" he shouted.

He waved the burning horror in the night sky. Now he was the long leg of a triangle.

Goran was the other. He had no feeling skin. But his filthy clothes stuck to something. Goran came toward Irene from a different angle. He was standing in the stirrups. He felt his legs tight against his horse. He kept his eyes on the middle point of the three, her blouse flapping back behind her. Frank came at her, south, and Goran rode at her from the north, farther away. One boy dead, the other stood watching, one hand behind his head clenching the tied rope.

He yelled, "Hey!"

It was totally absorbed. "Hey, Mommy!"

The tiniest voice in the world.

"*Caw.*" Frank's sword came at a cutting angle through the air with a whipping sound.

Irene saw the thin silver light, her eyes reflected on it, slanted and quick. She ducked. She was in her breath. She drew a red-line heart on the faded yellow horse that became lost in the field behind the old house. It lay there, the brush strokes of the heart faded, almost gone. Now, as she ducked, she felt aware of her body, heavy, her extremities coming off her. Her thoughts had no time to die; they floated off toward the dark, quirky side of the moon where quick-dead thoughts coagulate and become mountainous.

"Daniel," she'd said. "Daniel, put your arms here."

She felt the thickness, the black hair, the thinner bone running long when he turned his wrist. Her wrist had silver bands that moved their few inches, up and down. He held her down by her wrists.

"Daniel, I want a baby," she said. "Jesus, He'll give us a beautiful child. Like Him. Like He was."

They had one.

Daniel didn't like the idea of it being like Jesus; he felt wrong about it. They had two more. Jesus wasn't clearly on their farm. The baby girl died. The middle child, named

Adele, didn't seem right. He seemed old for a child, yet at
the same time, very slow, very dull. He ran away, even as a
small child. He had an unusual ability to sense where people
went, and being able to follow and find them. He watched
as his mother hugged her arms to herself diving below the
sword.

She had two arms, two legs, and two hanging breasts
that remembered the babies, and now, still full, they pulled
the triangle closer, all the way to her. She ducked down. One
arm held for a moment across her chest, the other flew above
her head. Words dribbled from her, down to the ground.
"Jesus, save me! Help me!" The thought ran through quickly;
the sword came down through her neck.

Goran came at her. The two men passed the bloody sword
with words so tiny on it, female, that no one could see. They
grunted, the horses shook, the air spit on them and the trees
held on tight to their places.

"Maw!" cried Adele. "I ain't a girl! Paw!"

Goran jumped from his saddle, from the horn, his hand
pushed off. Irene never expected this. Her arms were ex-
tended out, a Y-shaped woman, now with no head. He hit
down upon her. They buckled forward with the impact. He
held her body. He put his head between her shoulder blades.
He had loved a girl like this once, between her flannel blades,
soft. The smell; he had almost cried. He didn't look up now
to where her head would be. He held on like a baby, looking
in the blackness at his own slow-moving thoughts.

"Gore!" came through the farm air. "Hey, Gor-annn!
Look what he's doing!"

Fourteen men on horses watched. One stuttered and he
yelled with his mouth wide open, like his eyes. He was a

young man. Goran was meat. He ate anything he could catch. He lifted Irene's skirt to find the flesh. He spread her and opened her. He pushed into her. Her rear stroked up off the ground in the air. There was air between her and the ground. He pushed inside her, a headless woman. Irene, her heart stopped inside her rib cage, silent, held by the curved bones, like fingers. Her head was turned toward the two of them on the ground. It wasn't her anymore, not with Goran inside her. He rammed again and again as hard as he could. He reared up, his neck muscles straining red. His own head turned up to the sky. The cawing bird flew close to the tip of his nose. He felt the breeze of the spread, blue wings.

"Blue jay," he thought.

But it wasn't.

Gore was the bully in several childhood memories. Once he had a monkey on a rope at the top of the tree. He swung it high in the air and snapped its neck with a fall and a jerk. He swung his brother, Windy, by the arm and leg to fly from the farmhouse roof, to break. His own memory was a streaked yellow and a dark spitting taste in his mouth.

Goran snapped his teeth at the bird in the air.

"*Caw,*" screamed the man.

"*Caw,*" went the sound up high.

He went deep into the dead woman and screamed to the blue bird each time.

Frank Chaney watched. He never winced but once at the scene. It wasn't the headless body pumping blood from the horrible neck opening he had made. It wasn't Irene's severed head and twisted face. Her eyes were open and empty. It wasn't the screaming man inside her yelling at the birds.

That didn't bother him. Frank Chaney could even feel himself inside her dark opening where Goran was.

He winced when he saw who Irene changed into.

He saw her lying on her front side, head intact, as a little girl in a bright yellow day dress pulled up to allow a man inside. She held a little doll face to face with herself, the doll's head to the ground, taking the grinding into the dirt on the soft cotton back of her.

She spoke to the doll.

"Dolly, sweet baby," she said. "I'm sorry, little baby, I'm sorry."

Her legs were pulled thin, brittle-looking. She wore white socks. She had only one shoe on. Her legs were spread as far apart as they would go without breaking off. She took it, with her arms at her sides, buckling, her palms up to the sun. She twisted and struggled under Goran; her eyes stared up at Frank Chaney for help. When he did nothing, she turned her face in the other direction. He watched her neck, thin, white, and her backside bucking.

Frank Chaney felt himself sucked into where Goran was. He felt heat, extreme tension in his body, the horror and the awful smell, a death stuck up inside the deep chamber-silent tomb of the woman's body, a tunnel squeezing the breath out of him. There were brown colors and blacks; he thought he saw faces along the tunnel walls. Then he was back on his horse, sitting, watching. He put his hand down where he was wet in his pants. His face was sweat-soaked and white. He turned his face away from the dead woman.

"Don't!" he yelled. "Don't kill him! Stop!"

He saw his men had approached the boy at the pole.

"Don't go near him, I say! He's holy! Don't kill him or we'll all die!"

"Holy? You cut his mother's head off."

"Yeah, and Gore's over there fucking her."

"Holy, you say?"

"He is! Leave him alone!" Frank Chaney rode over close to the boy on the rope.

"Yeah, but you did it," someone said, "and now you're just scared."

"Look at his eyes," said Frank Chaney. "They're white. No color left, just the black holes. Leave him be. He's special."

"Get the food. Burn the house. We're not stopping here."

The boy moved behind the pole. He stared at the man on the horse near him. His white eyes cried. He started to run around the pole, around and around. There were the cawing screams. Around and around, in and out. The sun came up and it would go back down, the moon would come out somewhere in the sky; it would get dark. Around and around, things went around in a circle.

"Do we need to get food for Goran?" one man said. "Or is he going to eat that woman you killed?"

They rode from the farm into the wilder land, then to other farms, but nowhere was it like here, with Irene and the boys. Similar, but not the same. They wore their bloody hands. Frank Chaney and Goran, and Bobby, who stuttered. They rode on. They spared the boy at the pole.

Holy.

WITH LIGHT

Adele got himself cut loose by the same blade that cut his mother's head off. Then he ran. He smelled his way. He followed. Nature led him into the envelope. His mother had danced in circles. Where the blood was, was where he headed. Where the blood was starting to cake. The living men dug graves.

He breathed the same air, crossed the same ground his father had.

"Papa," he thought, "Mama."

His eyes were white, blanched from the original blue. He smelled a creek nearby. He tried to avoid the death smell. He ran into a meadow. He started to cry, confused, but also like he'd arrived somewhere that he should. He felt his father nearby.

There were men gathered in the meadow digging a big hole and picking up things from the ground. Adele still had the leather strap around his neck. It flapped to remind him. He turned from the men, into the small woods. There he leaned against a tall tree, out of breath. He saw a man on the ground in a gray torn uniform. His heart beat hollow holes. He walked over to the man. He looked at the face, dead one day.

"Papa."

He saw how the knees were bent, the legs under him. He leaned down and put his face near his father's. He opened his eyes against the familiar face. He pushed against his father. He held him, he hugged him.

"Papa, I came to find you. I knew I would, that I could. Mama's dead. Two men killed her, and drug her down to the ground."

Adele looked at his father's torn and twisted clothing, his bloody chest and the hole ripped into it. He watched for his father's eyes to open, or move. He whispered and looked away.

"She didn't have her face anymore."

He saw another line dimly running into the woods. He got up. He stepped over his father's body. He thought about his father's wrists and about how it would feel to step bare-footed on them. The line was connected to a girl. He followed it.

She was turned over on her back. She had no shirt on. Her eyes were closed. He saw her chin, stuck forever in lines of a frown. He looked into the dark, open mouth where there seemed to be a little light, like a small match flame. Adele looked at the sunlight on the leaves and on her body. Her dress was torn, too, twisted around her body. Her face had blood on it. The bullet hadn't come through her face, but there was a gash in her forehead. He looked at her, downward. There was something there.

"It's mine." He said, "Give it." He touched her, and she wasn't soft. He pulled his fingers back. They moved down into her dress pocket to find it. The watch. He felt it ticking. He didn't even look at it. It was his, and he knew it, and he held it tight in his hand.

"Hey! Git away from there, boy! What are you doing?" Some men came up to him.

"He's just a farm boy," said one. The other man said, "He looks addled to me. Look on his neck. And his face. What do you do with a boy like this?" said the man.

He was tall and he had marks, scars, all over his face. "The war will ruin everyone. Nothing is the same anymore. Even the children."

Adele saw them bury the dead from the woods in the meadow. The grave was a hole in the middle of the green field. The dirt was turned, fresh and black. They piled many bodies into this one. Several went in before Daniel. He went down into the earth on his back. Only one female went in; she was young. She went into the hole facedown. The men saw her white back. She rested on Daniel.

"They were buried together," a man said.

Others were stacked on top. The men piled the dirt on. There was no flicker of a light emerging from the grave. People were buried in a hole in the ground together. Adele made a slow circle around the grave. A man took hold of his arm. A man held him there, then walked him away from it—where the silence wasn't so strong.

TEDDIANNE AND THE RED TRUCK; 1960

Someone was calling her back. Her image was in the mind of another. She was nameless, faceless, to the dreamer. She had been a last, deep impression to him—it itself was calling her back. It was manifested; it was making a form, like a map, for her to join.

She had rested. She had grown, and she had tasted the bright yellow, like gold. She tasted it in a wide place, free, almost formless, a heaven. She was nudged, gently taught, and she had been faced by something unknowable but irresistible. Now she was almost ready. She held on like always, at either end of the journey. She felt herself falling—then a tunnel where faces, figures, knowledge, were imprinted on the soft walls, storied.

A name, the sound, familiar, faded. The sharp cracking echo sound faded. Many different memories faded, each one complete.

She saw herself at a blackboard, her face twisted so no one could see. She sucked her thumb all day long. She became a girl, a dancer. She had been in a war. There was a man. She had been a war. There was the man. She remembered him. She had seen his face many times. He was calling her back.

Rolling through the tunnel lined with time, she moved toward a pinpoint of light. The point had red in it, then brighter, then something popped—that point was no longer a point but a place.

And when she, her, had entered her body, there was a mark, like a scar, from the entry, shaped like what she held in her hand, small and curved like a spoon-scar.

It stayed in her mind.

She found herself holding a spoon. Hearing: "Honey, it was so peculiar last night—did I tell you? I just thought of it, how it struck me. Getting the clothes in off the line last night in the dark. Usually I do it in the day, but I forgot last night and went out, and it was strange doing it in the pitch-dark. The shapes of the clothes themselves looked different. They didn't have shadows. They seemed more like—they were living things, but, now this is the scary part—it was so dark, it's so silly, but the clothes were like they didn't have something they should have had—" and she leaned closer to her husband, who was eating from a bowl, watching the back of a box. She whispered something.

You bang on the table, and on your bowl of food, and the other one, the sister-one, touches you. She looks like the other one, but smaller, and says, to your face, "Don't," to your inside-hearing in your head, which is shaped to be you and at a certain thickness of skull. You can put your hands there on its warm sides.

You hear as you beat the bowl: "Don't, Teddianne." So you say, "Don't." And they all go to pieces.

DADDY

Teddianne had a circle tattoo, but not yet on. Its turning was there but not yet seen or known by her. The tires on their car had white circles that spun. The family made trips in the car. They raced through the tunnels that Teddianne liked.

Sometimes they drove in the early fall to avoid the summer's heat. At the gas stations were rain puddles with gasoline floating in colors on top. The breeze blew the colors around near Teddianne's feet on the gravel. She was waiting in her brown shoes that were untied. It was a triangle—the edge of the green car, her shoes, and the rain puddle.

The car had a face; it had a chrome grill around it; it was rounded in back. Teddi put her hand there and felt the curve and its big feeling. They were like a star, the family, the five of them together. Teddianne carried a pocket watch. She held it tight in her hand when she looked at its face. Her own face made you stop, to look at it.

The gravel gas stations had cafés. The car became quiet, the doors opened, and there would be a little breeze. Teddianne sat with her white thin legs sticking out the side door.

She waited for her daddy to come out with a bag of food, a cigarette in his mouth.

He drove the car badly, wild, too close to the other cars. His elbow rode out of the window, but he always told them about his friend, Oscar Poole, who got his arm knocked off like that when a bus came too close to the car he was in— and not to do it—but he did it. He was smiling, and smoking, and eating.

He'd say, "Mama, give me that short," and he'd smoke it and he'd look over his shoulder or into the rearview mirror and say, "Look over there, there's an ape driving a car," and they would look but never saw an ape, but a black man, and they felt sometimes, like then, that the backseat was miles away from the front, when Mississippi was slow, and hot, and the people lived there together, separately. It smelled like whiskey and had corn growing.

"Okay, who wants to be the Yankees? Someone has to be the Yankees. Charles, you'll be the Yankees this time. It's your turn."

"No, Daddy, I want to be the Rebels. I'm always the damn Yankees."

"Charles!" said Mama.

"Oh, Mama, it's okay when it's about the Yankees."

"Well, anyway, I'm the South," said Teddianne.

She had blue eyes, and her hands were at her chin, propping. She watched Charles with a side glance, cutting her eyes.

"You were the last time. Now I am," said Teddianne.

They played a Civil War game inside the green car, moving. The cornfields on the left were the Rebels, and on the right, the Yankees. The fields ran parallel with the car, going down the thin highway in between. The corn was tall, and green, and sometimes ran way back to the horizon or over a rolling hill, curving out of sight. The kids hung out the windows, measuring how big their sides were.

"Look, y'all. My side's way bigger than Charles's, isn't it, Daddy? I win. I beat the damn Yankees sure—huh, Daddy?"

Teddianne had a purr in her throat, in her voice. It rubbed everybody right. She said, "Daddy," and her daddy rode up in front at the wheel with his big head. Her sister, Sandy, rode up front in silence. Sometimes Daddy would pat her on the leg below where her shorts were rolled or nudge her in the side with his elbow. She'd put her eyes to him but usually rode eyes straight ahead on the road or half-closed.

"Yeah, Ted's right. Her field's much bigger, Charles."

They saw the armies marching, blue and gray, bayonets and silver buttons shining in the sun, and their fighting stained the yellow corn red.

"Charles, you don't have to lose, you can still win. It's only one battle."

Daddy'd give Teddianne a side smile, with his two-day whiskers on.

"Just keep a lookout, that's all. Don't fall out of that window."

They passed a white billboard.

"That sign said about Jesus," said Charles. "It was about building a house somewhere."

"Build your house on rock, not on the sand," said Mrs. Sayers. "Do you know what that means, Charles?"

"Yeah, I guess so," said Charles, "I mean, yes, ma'am."

He slouched down in his seat by the window.

Mrs. Sayers repeated the whole thing about the rock and

the sand. She had her Bible with her. Then she thought about
Christ and His garment. "Just to touch it," she thought, "and
be made whole, and healed." She read out loud in the car
while they rode on the two-lane—in the middle of the children's game.

"Y'all listen now. 'And whithersoever He entered into
villages, or cities, or country, they laid the sick in the streets,
and besought Him that they might touch if it were but the
border of His garment: and as many as touched there were
made Whole.' "

"What's that mean, Whole? You mean like a hole, or
what?" said Charles.

Teddianne reached over and put her hand over Charles's
wrist, around it at his cuff. She looked out the window.
Teddianne saw a blue ribbon caught in a barbed-wire fence,
blowing near the green grass. The colors caught her eye; she
smiled at the corners of her mouth. She was soothed by its
blowing. She thought of the color white and of His garments
that made Whole. At home was the red scarf cloth on the
gate—blowing, too.

In the mornings, they traveled early, sleepy, the windows
rolled up. It could be cold in the fall. Teddianne sat low by
the right-hand, Yankee window. She drew lines on the cold
window with her finger. Sandy rested her head in her daddy's
lap, her sock-feet all the way over to the passenger door.
Mama sat in back, Charles in the middle, sleep-faced.

"Look there," said Teddianne, "at the horse. He's up
early. He was standing back there," and she leaned up and
around to watch it. "He had his thick brown coat on and he
was half-white. He was breathing. You could see it, Mama—

the breath came out of him. I saw it. Coming out of his nose and his mouth. He's got two colors, and he's alive."

"Of course he's alive, Teddianne."

"No, but he's Alive."

Teddianne took a slow, deep breath and held it, then poured it out.

"He's alive in that big field and I saw him."

Her hands went up to her mouth as she pressed on her upper lip. The car was silent, with just the air streaming by.

"Roll down the windows," said Harold Sayers. "Roll them down."

"It's too cold," said Sandy. "I'm sleeping."

"Roll them down. It'll wake us up. It's time to wake up. Look around, the sun's up."

It was shining white on the hood.

"Open the windows and let her in, Teddi, Mama, come on." Harold Sayers rested his hand on Sandy's head in his lap, and their breaths could be seen, fast, like thin clouds. It ran together from the five of them and they were together, one whole piece.

Teddianne saw it, and, closing her eyes, she felt herself rising, rising in herself, upward, above the car, and the rising had a rose color to it and a smell, and there were hands that lifted her. They rode together in the car, the sun coming in the windows, mixing with the cold. The horse was way behind them now, and Teddianne started to cry. The moment that was like a rose color had changed; it smelled different now, bad, like death, and worse, like deaths. She cried tears that ran down her cheeks in lines. She was up above the car. The deaths smelled rotten. It got dark to her. She saw Sandy swelled up like a pale balloon, creased. She saw her daddy, changed. She saw Charles falling down.

"Daddy," she cried. "Mama."

"What's wrong, baby?"

Her mother touched her on the arm and on her face with the tears and Teddianne felt something go out of her; she came back inside herself in the car. Her hair was blowing back from the windows, showing her delicate neck, the fine lines of her face, and the softness of her throat. She turned her face to the side.

"Let me out, please. Let me out of the car. I have to stop, *now*. Daddy!"

The car pulled off the highway onto the fine gravel on the side. Teddianne flew from the car down a road bank and over a thin ditch into the woods close by. The car sat with one door open.

"Mama, oh, Mama," she cried. "Charles." She cried into her hands, her back against the tree. "Don't, Daddy, don't. Oh, Sandy, oh, don't." She pushed her hands into the dirt, clenching her fingers together and she clawed at the cool blackness.

She was such a young girl to have seen what she had seen.

IMPRESSIONS

The night Teddianne was born, in 1952, her mama had the white light. It stuck to her thighs, it was a home birth. Her thighs were like milk with a flashlight ray. The white light came from inside her. The lights were on in the bedroom, so no one noticed. The light came from the child.

"She was born with teeth," said her mother. Her Bible had fallen to the floor. "I'm calling her Monkey. I expected her to have a tail, she was in me so long. I know she didn't want to come out." Her mother, drenched and faded, intense with her black hair stringing wet, held the little girl.

"Where's my Bible?" she asked. She had a religious, squashed-looking face. Her nose and mouth looked too close together. The baby made sucking faces and little popping noises with her mouth, while her mother swished her hand along the floor. "I need the Book. I want to name her."

With one hand Mrs. Sayers felt the suture holes in her baby's head; soft, quiet pockets like warm glass.

A young neighbor lady that sat in a wallpapered corner of the room had her trained eye on the child. "It's like she was pulled right out of forever or somewhere. There's a silence on her. Why don't you name her Quietly? Or what's a good name for quiet things? Can you hear me, Helen? I feel like we're in a tomb or somewheres."

Her father had been on the front porch for thirteen hours, waiting for the child to be born, noticing the smallest movements of day and then night, the currents from the porch. As he came into the house, he thought of her conception in the Gulfport motel room, cold wet bathing suits and sand, where the drinking water tasted so bad. He stood above their bed now, looking at his baby. She had dimples above her little hips. The attic fan blew hot air and cicadas.

"We ain't calling her Monkey. Or Quietly. Or any Bible name, either. I've been thinking out there. We'll call her Teddianne, after my father." He saw his wife holding the Bible with one hand and the baby with the other, her hand wrapped around the back of its head. "Better spell it right for a girl, with an 'i.' "

He had two little girls now, the firstborn being Sandra. She was a tall girl with thin eyes and thin lank hair. She almost died once, when she got lost at her father's bakery. She climbed up and fell into a vat of flour that covered her except for the top of her hair. She jumped up and down on tiptoe the best she could with the white weight holding her, until a man working nearby happened to look into the flour vat. The top of her head looked like Teddianne's head coming out from between her mother's legs—all that white light preceding her.

Harold Sayers held on to his little girls after that.

When Teddianne was little, when she used to squat down, playing in the grass, Harold Sayers would put a huge hand on her back, supporting her, feeling her life underneath.

He claimed to have seen her future on the back of his hand, outlines in the blue veins. Pictures of what was to be—little colors of time. The blood turned red while he watched it, he said, and his face did, too. He snapped his eyes shut and some tears squeezed out the corners. In anger, he yelled out to the long backyard, "It's a lie, dammit—just a dirty lie!" He yanked his big hand away like it was hot there, like he had burned his hand onto her back.

He yelled at Sandra, standing nearby under a tall tree, "Git over here to me. Something might fall down and hit you on the head. Just stay close to me from now on."

He told his wife he had intuitions about the girls—that maybe they had lived before as sisters, that he had had a vision about their past, and that they hadn't had an easy time of it. "It was all red, and dark. I saw the moon as an evil thing, and Sandra shaking and hiding, and Teddianne clear out of her mind."

He made it up, she thought.

But he was afraid to even remember all of what it was he'd seen.

"That's not right, Daddy," said his wife.

There were pictures of that young time. Backyard shots of the three of them together. Daddy was huge, Teddianne stood up to his knee, and his wild hair was fully blown, caused either by the wind or his frame of mind.

Beautiful, and outspoken, Teddianne inherited her family's knack for making impressions. When she was twelve, her brother, Charles, was killed when he fell to earth from fifty feet of tree—floating as he fell with his arms stretched wide and a towel flapping behind him. He hit with a heavy sound, and the sound made a place like a spoon shape in

Teddianne's heart. Sometimes later, Teddianne used to come
and sit near to that deep impression in the ground. She ate
lunch there sometimes in its dwell.

Her father worked in the bakery where Sandra almost died
in the white. His job was to take the hot loaves from the oven
on racks, spin around and place them on cooling tables behind
him. He did that for seventeen years. After he retired, some
men noticed a smooth indentation in the bakery floor, where
Harold Sayers had pivoted his shoe over the years.
    In concrete.

Teddianne's mother had been hit by a shovel in a riot over
the sexual consent laws in the state of Mississippi. She wore
it pretty well, and it was Teddianne who later inherited her
mother's slanted face. As a child, Teddianne was silent,
almost mystically inward. Later, she would talk, sideways
through her wet, red lips, and her eyebrows would lift up for
extra emphasis.

After her brother was dead, Teddianne sat in the backyard.
She sat in the leaves—they were red ones—making her think
about Charles falling from the treetop. He was like the leaves
falling, wearing his red corduroy shirt that fell in the air,
until it hit down. She sat still and looked at the red falling
in the air. It reminded her of other times; her mind like a
long barrel reached backward and only saw space, lighted.
She was like a pyramid, big on the inside.

She remembered Charles's small white hands and scraped knuckles, and Sandy asked her only once, "How do you get into that ocean place, inside, Teddi?" And Teddianne answered, "You stop."

That was where they were so different.

JESUS AND THE TATTOO

Teddianne sat still in the leaf rain, watching Sandy walk slowly up the hill to the back door of the house. Sandy was bigger, she looked like a woman, at fifteen. Some of the colors were in Teddianne's hair and some brown ones stuck in Sandy's as she walked. Teddianne was on her side, on her hip, and her dress curved under her, soft.

She and Charles used to slide down the steep hill to the college on big cardboard pieces. Running up to the gray cement wall with the small, indented windows that had the thick glass that you couldn't see through. One time Teddianne left her little pocket watch in one of the windows there, and it sat there all winter long. She and Charles went and got it the next spring when they remembered, and it still worked. She thought of him and how he had a pointy face. She looked at the ground through where her fingers were spread out. A purple leaf hit and stopped near her. The little hem of her white dress was undone and stuck down in places uneven. She had a tattoo on her stomach. It was a circle, thick as a rope, and it looked like it was turning. When she sat like this, it was wrinkled in the folds of her skin. The tattoo was in the middle of her stomach. The tattoo man said, "It'll hurt on the stomach; that's a tender place. The needle'll hurt."

"A tender place," Teddianne said. "That's nice."

It hurt, it pinched, sharp little pains rising to her head. She gritted her teeth. She pictured the colors squeezing out the end to become drops. She thought of Charles when it hurt the most. He had been gone a long time, almost two years. The years went out of her like cold things, pale and watery. She watched the color going onto her skin making the picture.

The man worked his needle along the circle while Teddianne looked around the room, turning her head to see the walls, with the illustrations. It was so quiet in the room, Teddianne could hear the creaking of her neck bones. Then it was whiter inside the circle than it had been before.

The circle went on at night; it was an infinite thing.

She was thirteen when she got it.

"Thirteen. That's a great age for a girl. It's got color to it. I don't remember being thirteen. I was twenty before I got a tattoo. I shouldn't give you this, you know. Your age; it's illegal. You might change your mind later and then what?" But he liked her, and he liked the circle idea, and the colors she wanted. "Thirteen."

"I'm not too young, though," she said. "I've seen almost everything. I've even seen the insides of my body—the organs in there and their colors—purples and reds, mainly. I wanted to get color put on my outside now. Inside and out, the same. Even when I'm dead, the circle will be there. Under the ground and the grass and if it snows; even if I was buried in the center of the earth, it would still be there. I wish Charles had one. I want one for him."

"Who's Charles?" the tattoo man said. "Your friend?"

"No, he's my little brother," Teddianne said. "He's dead. He fell out of a tree."

"You've got bird bones," he told her. "Your little wrists, your hands. Your neck is so pretty. Come here." She got down and walked to him in the yellow light of the room. "You're so little." He kissed her on the head. She was like a light, glass thing to him. His arms were huge, printed with colors like the funny papers. He kissed the other side of her head. He was so fat he was filling the room.

She said, "It'll be different from everything else that ends."

She told the tattoo man, "This is for me and Charles and Sandy. Jesus said, 'Men may come and go, but I go on forever.'"

The man looked at her. He swallowed in his throat, liking her.

He said to her, "I didn't know He said that."

"He did."

The winds blew the red scarf cloth and the throat sounds at night.

"She touched His garment and was made Whole."

Whole. Teddianne was a shut-in with a circle tattoo. She learned to listen.

"Yeah," Teddianne said. "The lady touched Him from behind, just on the hem of His garment, and it healed her. It stopped her bleeding to touch Him. I saw Him at our house. My mom was dying in bed in the living room. I told her I saw Him there with her. She believed me."

The tattoo man's eyes were a deep-water blue, like parts of his hands, and he watched her.

She pulled up her thin shirt. "I only saw part of Him, actually," Teddianne said.

The tattoo man said, "Now this will hurt when it cuts in. I'll be careful with you. You tell me how it feels, and don't tell anyone about me doing this, you understand?"

Teddianne thought, "I've seen people die. In my mind. I'm not a little girl anymore. Not since a long time."

She said to the man, "I understand."

The tattoo man worked quietly in the yellow light. Her little body held her purple organs. Her chest was white with small breasts, at thirteen a symmetry to them, and their redness, with soft subtle curves outward. He touched her with his hands, into the night. And then she left, and went home with a bandage on her stomach. Her fingers felt her way into the house, to her room in the dark, to her bed, alone. She prayed in her bed that looked pale white in the dark, on her back, facing upward. She held her hands together in front of her face in the air.

"Dear Father, help me understand. I love You, that's all I really want to say and to feel. I feel You all the time inside, as a big clean space. Help me to know how it's right what they do and what I do. Help me to do what You want me to do. And Daddy."

She was quietly aware of herself in her bed, in her house, in the land around it—the gate with the red ribbon.

"I'm here. In Mississippi, God."

She felt bigger than her house, than her town, than the world—inside was much bigger than that. No size at all, then, unbounded.

"Father, I love You so much. This feeling, the silent

space of you. I want my heart to be like this all the time for everybody in a real way. Our Father Who art in heaven, show Yourself to me. God Bless the fat man tonight, and Mama and Daddy and Sandy and Charles and all the animals everywhere in the world. And Jesus."

She slept, her eyes moving under the lids. Sometimes she could hear the wind in the trees or the gate squeaking in back, and the stairs. Some nights Sandy came in with her, and would get in, and Teddianne would hug her around the waist.

THE STOP PLACE

Little girls, dancie, in front of the mirrors; their bare feet on the bathroom rugs, skittish. Their naked, white bodies, so thin, and their stomachs stuck out. Teddianne and Sandy took baths together. They took turns sitting under the water in front. Before, they had been able to both sit up front together, side by side, under the rushing, hot water that caused even their little minds to settle down, and think.

Teddianne wore sunglasses with red rims, in the tub. She rested her face on her knees with her front teeth. She told Sandy, "Sometimes I'm not me. I slow down inside—and it's white all around. Everything stops. It takes a while to get going again. It's a stop place."

She sucked the water from her knees. The water was sweet there. The ends of their hair were wet, dark against their white, curved backs. They leaned down toward the heat. She sucked on the water from the washcloth.

"Does that happen to you, too, Sandy?"

"I don't know," Sandy said. "You shouldn't suck on that water, or you'll get polio, Mama said."

Already, as a child, Sandy's face had a peculiar slanted look. And her legs were bowed.

Teddianne kissed Sandy's wet back.

"That's not true," said Teddianne, and she took off her red sunglasses. "I saw Jesus in the living room with Mama."

"That's not true. Him and God are invisible, no one can see them."

"Mama believed me. He put His hands on her head. He was gentle, Jesus."

She rode herself back and forth, making waves. The water held their hands and legs and colored toys that floated. They sat on the white porcelain together.

"Did you really see Him?" asked Sandy. She was staring down into the water. She saw her legs where the blue veins ran through her thighs.

"Yeah. Mama's gonna die soon, I think. Jesus looked at me, until I forgot who I was."

Sandy leaned back and Teddianne held her around the waist, resting her face on her wet shoulder.

"Teddi. I don't know about all that, and Mama. But we'll always be sisters, won't we? We'll be the same, together. I want to be like you."

The girls sat and felt the heat and the closeness and the cool air on top. They were seeds, so different—the same, but grown different.

They had been a family. They had dogs in the doghouse. They had a yard and a woods nearby. And they weren't lying. They were with each other. Their father had a prickly face.

His lips were like Teddianne's; he kissed her. They lived without thinking about it, in a house, on a street, on a hill, in a time that was slow and South, and hot, with a peace and a yellow calm.

Teddianne sat in the backyard while her mother worked in the yard. She hung the colored and the white clothes up to dry in the breezes. Teddianne began to read. The family slowly began to become separate people. Sandy stood and watched after the swing hit Teddianne in the face. Blood seeped through her teeth, her lips were cherry red. Tears rolled down by themselves without any sobbing. Sandy watched her place a curled hand around the steel swing-set bars—a small, white, grasping hand—and then sit down. Her white shirt was stained red from the blood, and black from the dirty tears. Her father ran down the hill.

"What happened to her?"

Sandy watched how he loved Teddianne best. Then she watched the green wall come at her and go back and forth, and there had been her blood, a new red, flowing out in pain onto the Christmas box. Daddy was her first love. Then there were more, and Teddianne hid in the closet, and in her books, then in her mind. That's where Teddianne learned to hear and learned to be able to see like how she came to see the red truck for what it was.

Sandy spilled her blood over the footlocker—and even though she cleaned it off, it was always there. Inside the box were the lights, and the flashers—purple and red, blue, yellow, gold, and green. There was silver tinsel, and small angels in the dark box. It was being pushed. She was over it. There was a statue of Santa Claus and the reindeer. Santa's porcelain bag was open and empty but for flakes that looked like tobacco. Sandy's head almost touched the green wall. She put her hands up against it, together, in front of her face, and her forehead touched there. At Christmas time, they always had that box out. Now she was bleeding over it. He bent her that way, and her heart. Later, there were others, the boys who smelled it. Once there were seven, laughing, and her face was twisted.

Teddianne was up in the closet in the pitch blackness. She waved her hands in front of her face to try to see them. She listened to the birds that sang—then, farther away, singing softer to her. The train was downstairs in the day with Sandy, in and out of her.

There was one day at the family house on Washington Street, in that summertime when the magnolia and the mimosa were burning the air with scent, when Teddianne and the rest of them were in the front yard. They used to swing off the second-story porch of the white, wooden house in a tire swing erected years ago by Charles.

Teddianne was swinging high, Daddy was smiling through it all, with his hands on his hips, a cigarette in his mouth, his eyes on Sandy and on the soft, summer day. Mama was outside; she was spitting out some blood from recent dental work, into the dust at the base of the big oak tree. Sandy was standing, empty, watching her sister in the air. Sandy was the only one paying attention when the rope broke with Teddianne up high in the air. They heard the snap; their separate thoughts vanished in the air. They stretched out their arms upward. They focused their eyes, ready, seeing Teddianne's legs blown visible from under her flapping cotton dress. They waited. And then they waited, and she hung there, just a little too long. It seemed in that time that the breeze and the blowing trees stopped. The cars traveling down Washington Street stopped. The blood in their veins, the air inside their lungs, stopped. Teddianne was in the air.

She stayed that way, in the air.

Then she hit down in their midst, lightly, on her cotton behind. They were a small band, a circle, around her. She looked up at their faces, her family. Sandy was scared, gray-faced, already gone, already missed. Mama understood what couldn't be understood. Her daughter had already seen Jesus and told her so. Mama was on her way out, too, already gone. Her father had the sun bouncing off his bare head. His hands stayed on his hips.

He said, "What did you do? Tell me, Teddi, what did you do?"

Sandy looked at her father with the same question.

"Teddi. What did you do?"

And Teddianne was the sum of them. Her rays went out and touched. She knew the difference between what was and what was not. The circle around her vanished; the circle that was on her stayed and kept going.

Sandy gave birth to a deformed baby. Sandy was sixteen.

Teddianne listened to the neighborhood kids—they gathered around the doorjamb. They looked in, whispering, "It's a water-head baby."

The baby lay in its bed with its mother for a short time before it died. The hall was empty, the doorjamb quiet in its pale, orange wood.

Sandy lay on her side-face and cried for her life and for the big-headed baby and for the father. Soon after, she took the bus out of town with a boy from the box factory. He was dirty and hardheaded. He wasn't the father. They left in an early gray light, her belly scarred, the stitch lines still very clear, from her being cut open like a melon; that big, dying baby coming up out of her swamp of fears, all of them coming true.

Sandy rode the bus out of town with the boy. She pulled at her thin hair, to make it grow. In the bus smell and in the recent-death feel, sitting on the hard seat with a small-eyed boy, she thought no thoughts, and let the boy put his dirty fingers inside her, underneath the jacket on her lap in the dark as they rode in the nighttime. There were a few lights outside the black window at a distance. She could see herself in the reflection pulling at her hair. She told the boy, "Keep doing it. It feels good." She leaned her thin head back on the seat, sick inside herself from her stomach to her heart.

Teddianne watched them leave that day, from behind her curtain.

"Sandy."

She watched them carry their bags. Sandy's hands were red, with deep lines. The suitcases were black and swinging. Teddianne whispered words to herself, over and over, and the repeating of them drove out the sadness. She sat, with her eyes softly blue, and said: "Sandy, Sandy, Sandy, sandy, sandy, sandy, san, san, san, sss," and she was gone.

She stopped, where the colorlessness was beautiful. It stayed with her. She called herself "Teddianne," and she was sweet, and she covered everywhere the same like a soft rain.

She told her daddy, the only one left, she said, "Daddy, I've stopped in my mind. It's perfect. I love it, it goes on. It's myself. It's my heart. Don't you want to know me?"

But he was a stranger, the way he looked at her.

CHRIST

Teddianne ran out of the house from the back door and up over the front yard hill. Parked on the street was Christ. It looked like a red truck.

It sat, facing down the hill.

"It's too big!" she cried. "I can't get it in. It hurts; the truck, it's too big for my heart."

She pressed her hand to her chest.

But then Teddianne fit it in. She got it in. She opened up and got it in.

In the South, in the wintertime, the ground sometimes sparkles with the morning frost. It didn't snow very often and the thin white would be gone by noon. They shot off firecrackers and Roman candles around Christmastime.

One year Teddianne got the flying bird, with the painted face. One winter she got a tattoo put on. It would be there forever. One year she tied a long red ribbon to the wooden gate in the back, down by the shed. And one day, in the winter, when she came outside, she saw a red truck.

THE YELLOW HAT

I wanted to get a yellow hat. Someone had a bird, in there, in one of the cells. I heard it sing. Sometimes it made me sad in the quiet. I wasn't the only one. I always pictured him yellow, but I never saw him as a boy bird. I never wanted to see him.

I had pictures only of Suzanne on the cell wall to keep me company. In the winter, the pictures seemed to curl in the middle outward—maybe the wall shrank from the cold. In the summer, the picture fell from the wall that sweated, like me. It fell from one corner. I never taped it back up. It just hung that way from its angle.

A yellow hat. It came to me. It was like a light, one night when the bird was singing, and now I was going to get one. I didn't know birds could sing at night. I thought they slept under a cover on the cage. The man who had him must've taken it off so it would sing to him in the dark. I imagined the bird, yellow against the black night in the cell, and the man's thick fingers compared to the body of the bird. Inside, his little heart beat fast-red. His eyes must've been quick, and thin-lidded. I heard him singing even when he really wasn't.

I didn't dream of the girl, of her anymore, but she was still with me like she had been all my life. It was like she wasn't there, in the dream world anymore. I remembered how I loved her, as a child, my dreams of her. It reminded me of Mama K, who I thought of often. I remembered the time Mama K forgot to light the smelly air, and when she did, it burnt fast. Me and Ned laughed as her nightgown went to fire. She ran and screamed, then we hit on the fire that was red. Her hair went from red to pure white before she was twenty-five.

That was before; now I was getting out, after three years. I caught a ride in a black truck. We went down a faded highway, heading from near one town toward another one I'd never been to. The wind came in my open window.

I had been thinking of the past before that day, then in the truck, for three years. I had walked, talked, and eaten, without color. Sometimes there would be the yellow bird, and then the idea of that color to think about. The color yellow had been inside me all my life. Maybe it was the color of my soul, or like a color gauge—of how I was doing here on earth.

Prison had been a place for the past. The clouds of it hung everywhere, clearly the way things had been, sometimes changed for the better. The little things stood out in the long time, hundreds of men on their backs, long nights, almost all of them in the past or the future. The present was too cheap and gray; it itched.

I said the name, "Suzanne." I spoke it. As rituals became all-important, I spoke her name, sacred, near and to a certain space on the gray-green wall. I could sit near it then, and feel close to her. I acted up, I cried when they moved me. I walked by my old cell to be near her place. I rubbed the metal paint off the cot bars thinking of her, remembering.

And the man driving asked me, "You coming from that prison back there?"

"Yeah," I said. "I been there."

I left my cardboard suitcase by the road, taking certain things into my pockets.

I kept the knife.

"I don't want to pry, but I figured you were. It's your haircut, and your suit," and he smacked his mouth, stretched wide at how I was still sitting there and the truck tires were still turning. He had told me already how the tapping of my ring on the body of the truck bothered him, the rhythm of it, the repetition of things, that it gave him a head pressure.

"I mean, I figured as much. I picked you up pretty close to the prison road. My boy works up there, in the kitchen. He's a cook."

The man's eyes were red-rimmed, his hair was gray and thin, and he had neck creases like he'd tied wire around it, and twisted. His knuckles stuck out, white on the wheel. "He's a pretty good cook, too. You must've eaten his food."

"Yeah, I imagine I did," I said.

"What's your name?" he asked.

"Billy-Billy Jump," I told him.

"Oh."

I imagined I did eat the man's boy's food, touched by his hands that had grown in the man's wife's belly and had

touched this man's hands with his own and maybe even petted
the man in a downtown store until he had pushed the small
hand away.

I had lived, grown, changed, for three years in one
building—had done it all with and through the food that this
man's son's hands had touched, and I saw the long lines.
The line of people in their ancestral places all connected
with this man and the world, the rhythms of breathing, and
being, and dying, and the man-made faces resisting the repetition, of each change. I knew that he was trying to die, to
stay still in a moment.

I was still deep in the habit of remembering. I remembered myself as a boy and an image came, of rusty nails
sticking into my knees. I remembered the round, rusty holes
they made in me. I used to bend down on my knees in the
dirt, in the grass, and on the wooden floor. I felt the nails
going in and stopping because the heads were too big. Mama
K told me it was because of sin you think this way, but if
you ever did get a needle in you, it would not stop but would
go up the veins right to the heart and kill you.

We passed several signs in the truck that had Jesus on
them, His name, and words to do. There were barns and dirt
going by. Underneath was the earth and below that, deep,
was the core, smooth, made of cold iron. It was dark and
solid, quiet, but inside it was the oldest air in the world.

"I mean, what did you do to get in a place like that?
You don't look too old, you couldn't have been in too long,
were you?"

"I did some things, one after another. I ended up out
there. It's hard to separate it from other things, even though
they did."

In my head I saw the man lying with his eyes red where I had stabbed.

"They drove me out there in a government car. A green one."

I sat between two men who didn't speak to me. They talked and laughed with each other and to the men in front. It was wintertime when I went up. The windows were up and there was very little air. I got so tired, tireder than I had ever been. It was like I was no longer in the car. That's when I started remembering things, right then.

"This is the first car I been in in three years, since then. Truck. I don't already remember being there, hardly. I'm gonna get rid of it all," I told him.

We rode quiet a while. I told him, "I had a trial. It was all outside of me. There were words, and then I was gone. I put a man's eyes out with a stick."

I know he must have gripped the wheel then, but I didn't look.

I remembered seeing and being red all over that cabin so much I could hardly see the man I blinded as a separate piece from the rest of it. I remembered his eyes looking their last. Suzanne was in the corner, and I was swinging. She was way outside the red. Her legs—I remembered her legs were pulled up to her chest with her hands wrapped tight around them in a circle.

"Uh-huh. Yes, well, now you're out."

There were dead bees on the dashboard down in the crack at the windshield. It reminded me of Suzanne visiting me in the beginning, and the crack, the line that ran between her breasts when she leaned over to talk through the window to me; she wore homemade dresses with straps over her smooth shoulders. She made her breasts do that so I'd remember her in my single bed until the next time.

The truck ran by fields that reminded me of her. She was fading but still there. I didn't have her picture anymore. I remembered meeting her in a field we knew. I saw her from behind in a blowing dress, her hair all blown to one side. She was waiting and looking. I ran to her, my feet stepping through dirt and weeds and wildflowers. Each step made a sound that crushed hot and dusty.

I could get very close to her without her hearing because she was deaf in one ear. When she was younger, she had gone with a friend up to an outhouse and looked inside through a hole. She turned her head, laughing, whispering, and the boy inside stuck an ice pick into her hot ear, aiming for her blue eye. She turned her good ear toward people when they talked.

A YELLOW DOG

Pretty good corn crop this year, a lot of rain," said the driving man.

He had spit at the corners of his mouth. His lips were slightly peeled-looking, from biting. "Maybe you could get on at one of the farms here, at least for a while."

"Yeah."

In the lines of the man's forehead, I saw Suzanne in the cool dirt of a furrowed row, lying on her stomach, her backside at me, with her hair messy red brown, and her thin white neck showing through.

"She's gone from me, anyway," I thought. "A year since I heard from her, since she went off with him." I'd cried about it enough, about the loneliness. Stabbing that man in a wild cabin when it had been fall, the browns and oranges coming through the window, sticking to everything. I'd seen her legs high up. It was cool, clean air, and the blood was like a red cloth stuck in his head. It waved. Sometimes it was all I saw.

I leaned out the window into the wind. I saw myself in the small side mirror, looking until the wind made tears.

There were deep lines near my mouth and my eyes. I smiled, and when I did, I spread out like I used to inside, jumping around the farm, behind the same eyes, the air on me like now, I thought. Mama K had been there. I saw some of her lines on my face.

"Well, I can get you into town. We're 'bout in it now. There's a parade they're having here today. It's June 26th. Pied Piper Day."

Town drew near. We were in it, then a part of it—it became bigger.

I only heard catches of what the man was saying, about the day. Something German about the Piper, some folks being related to him. I thought it had only been a cartoon thing.

"So they have a parade to redo the whole thing. You'll see. People come from all over to see it. My boy was in it a couple of years running. He was a rat.

"Hell, even I been in it. I chased after the Pied Piper man himself. He led the rats and he led the children off to somewhere nobody'd been to before. That's why they never could find them—didn't know where to look. Somewhere where the mind of man could not go."

I saw the man look straight ahead with that one. He seemed to be turning the wheel too much to be going straight.

We passed a yellow dog with cuts on his crewcut-like body. He was close, I yelled, "Hey!" The dog looked up, then trotted away toward the green grass and then the yellow and the green blended together into streaks. I saw the city sign that said what looked like "Cuba" and the population eight thousand something.

Pulling in, I remembered when Mama K would give me

change to carry in my pocket. "Billy-Billy, honey, now you got something to rattle," she said.

Now I had some bills. I felt them through the pants pocket on my leg. It was like the girl I used to carry there. Somewhere I'd let her go, just gotten rid of her. She ended up dusty somewhere. It was like she got too big, too real. She became born from the dreams and my thoughts into being too real to carry her in my pocket anymore. She was a real person, somewhere.

I was still a boy. I still felt Mama K and I felt inside like I always had. I put my hand in my pocket and touched the bills with different fingers. I missed my smaller, younger self. I had changed, but I hadn't. Things around me had changed. I was older but I wasn't grown. Touching the bills, I looked out through the windshield. Out the window were the rats.

Rat-faces. They were dancing and waving. The trees of the town square were decorated. Lanterns and yellow paper were hung up, and other colors were strung on the buildings. At a distance I could see a group of small people. It must have been children, but they didn't seem like children—they moved funny. But it was just that I hadn't seen children for a long time, and that I hadn't given that a thought until now.

We got closer in. I saw rat-faces all over the streets and waving with both arms at us to pull over. We were driving into the parade. The man and me and the black truck were in the parade. I slouched down, hugging the window, cutting my eyes, looking out.

Someone was gently pounding on the hood of the truck and yelling to pull off the road. Words came at us through a

rat-face. The mouth moved some when he yelled. The yeller
had an old blue mark on his arm. "Pull it over there! You're
in the way of the parade!"

I wanted to get out of the truck, into the town, and get
my yellow hat. I wanted a big yellow one with two bills, one
in the front and one in the back, too. This town; I wanted to
laugh at it, but I was scared to. I wanted to leave my self in
the old black truck and let it go, leave me in there and start
over, younger again, here in what sounded like Cuba—Cuba,
Mississippi.

I took my bag out with me, one step down first. I slammed
the door, rattling the window. The man looked at me. He
didn't move to get out. He was parked. Maybe he would just
sit and eat a sandwich or something his boy made him, and
watch the tail end of the parade.

People were running in every direction, wild. There were
gaps where there weren't any people, just light or grass, or
sky. At the far end of one long hole of air was the trailing
off of the kid group looking stiff and tied to each other by a
rope.

I gave the truck a quick good-bye. I wanted to back off
and run fast away, but I couldn't. I saw the man's eyes. I
slowed down inside. I tightened myself up some. I pulled my
pants up better by my belt with my one free hand.

"Thanks," I said.

I was standing in the grass by the curb. It wasn't going
to be that easy, to be back, to be young. I could see people
through his side window running and jumping in their outfits,
some of them rat-people, others just dressed up wild.

I saw bare legs, prancing. Someone was covered just

halfway and their legs stuck out below. I wanted to get rid of my own outfit. I watched the bareness go by. "I could never wear one of those short ones," I thought, maybe a rat-head or a rat-face, but not with my legs sticking down.

I felt like going to a bathroom to get rid of my black coat. It was too hot, it was bad clothes. "Girl," I thought. "Girl legs." I would take off my pants, too, in the bathroom of a bar, and touch myself. I could think about the legs and her body who wore the costume out there. I remembered the cot in my cell. I curled up with myself on it, holding and working myself toward a little peace in my body, until it would start again.

But instead of finding a bathroom and doing it, to relax, to calm down the images—of the hands, the legs, the rest of her—instead of getting it all over the inside of the coat, where the lining should have been silk, and stuffing it and the past three years into the toilet and watching it cover wet and disappear—I took off my coat, took my things out, put a couple of things back in, and pushed it down into a trash can made of wire there on the sidewalk. I stood above it. It was black and mashed, ruined in a wire cage. In my shirt-sleeves, I walked down the way, carrying my bag.

I went down the white sidewalk. I heard somebody yelling by my ear.

"Menlo! Menlo!"

I turned back to see what a Menlo was. I thought it could be part of the parade, but it was someone's name, being yelled by two other people, short people. They were throwing something Menlo wanted over his head back and forth. Menlo sprang up to get it and I could see his stomach when his shirt went up. He saw me looking when he hit the ground. He jumped again and again and pulled at his shirt in the air to keep it down.

"Menlo," they yelled. "Hey, Menlo!"

It was something bright red they were throwing. Whatever it was, he wanted it bad. I moved along with a group that pushed me my direction. I kept looking back.

There were tables out in front of the stores. It was the Pied Piper sale day. Half price. I'd never heard of this town, Cuba. I was almost three hundred miles from my hometown. Going there was a distant but definite plan. I didn't want to think about it yet, about going up to the house, or by the fields, and Suzanne's house. My parents were still there, in the house we grew up in, where Ned died in the backyard next door.

My hand jumped back off a copper pot my fingers were touching. It was new and shiny. I moved down to another store, with music playing. I stood near the open door and listened. There was a song on by a woman. Her voice was deep and tough. She was throwing it around. It was bouncing all over the store. Her voice broke, making short words longer. I went inside to look for her face on a picture somewhere.

I didn't want to ask. I put my bag down on the floor. Most of the people were outside in the parade. I moved through a couple of aisles. When the song went off, they didn't put on another one.

They watched me; it made me nervous. I remembered my bag and went back to it. On the cloth handles was a torn rat-mask. I brushed it off. It had a busted string and a slice down the forehead part. It looked at me. I picked it up quickly and stuffed it in my bag. It was my first new thing to have.

I imagined it strapped to my face looking out a window in a house, at people on a street. That felt all right to think about, but then it made me feel alone.

I had nowhere to go.

I was the only person like me, and in this town. I felt thinner than I should be, to their eyes, so thin like a reed, so thin as to not be there except as a spoiled sort of wavy thing.

I got down to a clothing store, with the mask in my bag with me. The town was clearing out some by now, maybe following the leader over a river to a woods somewhere. My thoughts were streaming through me in lines. I saw some hats through the store window. No rats. I also saw some people watching me from across the street. They had been walking along with me on the other side. I noticed them over there but not as much as I normally would have. I went inside where a bald man was cleaning the lint off another man's coat.

THE YELLOW HAIR

Teddianne Sayers was moving along the street across from the man carrying the bag. She'd dropped a broken rat-mask onto his carrying bag in the record store. She had seen him playing with his black jacket, taking things out and putting them back in. Then he stuffed it in the trash can. He acted funny, and he walked in a teetering way down the sidewalk, so she followed him.

She had a slight limp in her left leg, and she noticed the way he walked. She thought, "Like limping in both of his legs. Either that or he was lifting his feet up, both too quick, like the pavement hurt his feet."

She had noticed it, but it was his face she liked. It was nice, to her. His eyes were a little narrow, but not like slits. They looked light blue. His nose was normal-looking, she thought, "not like mine." His hair was cut short but grown out some. She wanted to come up to him and put her hands on the sides of his head.

She had been in the library that morning, reading about the life of J. E. B. Stuart. She became bored with the reading. Her head hurt her like it did much of the time. It felt like something was in her chest or her neck like a block, like the time she swallowed an ice cube and it stuck in her throat. Her father made her drink hot water that burned her lips. She looked out the library window and saw the man in the truck get stuck in the tail end of the Pied Piper parade. Then she sat on the sidewalk curb with her back against a sign pole. She drew in her knees to prop her elbows on.

"Teddianne, Teddianne," she thought.

Her name was what she liked best about herself, and some memories of when she was younger. She had been changed, broken some from an accident, and she missed certain feeling and parts of herself that she thought were gone.

"Teddianne," she said. "What's wrong with you?"

When she saw the man, she remembered clearer the feeling she thought she had lost. Something about him stuck out at her, made her feel the lost silence. It was an open, lit-up feeling of a larger place inside. She held her arm to her chest. She put both arms there, crossed.

"Teddianne," she said to herself.

Her face was a little crooked if it was seen straight on, but only at first, then her details stood out, and the slanted look went away.

Her face was pale-colored and small, her fingers often at it, and her hair was a straw-colored blond, cut short and ragged. It lay on her neck like a boy's, grown out some, emphasizing its thinness. Her hair and her neck were close-colored, and when she put her fingers there, just underneath, against her neck, there were three palenesses that shaped a silence and glowed a soft light, gentle as she sat on the white sidewalk, watching.

She looked like a very young girl, thirteen or fourteen.

She was sixteen years old.

Like her face, the rest of her was built in smallness. There was even a beauty in the way her clothes wore on her, small-pretty. She dressed like a boy, and underneath the folds of her shirt on her stomach, where it was flat and tender, was a circular, bright-colored tattoo that looked like it was turning.

"Teddianne," she spoke to herself.

She was a pale, curved little person, out there on the sidewalk, her one hand up to her face and one in close by her chest.

"He looks like he's lost himself."

Billy-Billy Jump tried on a yellow cloth hat. He looked at his reflection in the store window. He saw her out there in his second layer of sight, another, but pure, yellow.

SECRET
TOWN ROAD

Billy-Billy now had three colors on him—black shoes and pants, a white shirt, and the yellow hat.

It was a woman's hat, originally. Billy-Billy got it, used. He just liked the color of it. It had a long narrow bill that sloped down and out from his head, and the top, the top-hat part, was a flimsy cotton that actually met and tied in the back. Some dark hair stuck out in the back in the hole created by the tying of the two yellow pieces of cloth. The yellow hat rode gentle and light on his head.

He had paid twenty-five cents for it.

He walked out into the sunshine on Pied Piper Day, June 26, 1968. The rats had scattered mostly by now and even the girl who had glowed yellow sitting across the street was gone.

Billy-Billy moved down the street, thinking about what he was going to do. He walked. His feet moved in a rhythm, repeating. He thought of the man in the black truck. He had been in the truck a long time. It was the transition time; point. He remembered the man's side-face, how it had been reddish, and twisted-looking, when he looked and saw himself in a barbershop window. The colored pole was by the door with its swirling look. Billy-Billy saw his yellow hat, again in a window. It looked even brighter now.

"How do I look?" he thought. Then he said it out loud, and he felt the yellow color come down from his hat and cover his face and the back of his neck. He walked down the street, weaving slightly, his head feeling yellow.

He drifted out of town. He got a bottle of beer in a liquor store. Across the street was a vacant lot. There were two men talking and drinking from their bottles. He felt their hands on the long bottlenecks, and the cool, paper-wrapped part. The men were black; Billy-Billy thought about how their hands were whiter on the inside, on their palms.

Beyond the men was a field with an old, faded yellow school bus parked in it. There were brown weeds up to its black tires. Billy-Billy stood, watching the scene, standing near the red Liquor sign. The dirt was brown and the grass over there was green. It was a stuck moment. He stopped in the picture he saw and was in. He wanted it to stay like that, stopped. No more moments, like the man in the truck.

One of the men in the field lifted his head to look back at Billy-Billy.

"That hat looks terrible."

Billy-Billy turned around, but not before he felt a light hand tap him on the back.

"Awful," she said.

He turned and looked her in her blue eyes.

She pulled back some and squinted her eyes slightly.

"Who are you, to say that to me?" Billy-Billy said.

"I saw you come here, and saw you when you bought it."

She could feel the inside of him, how it was holding back. She nearly reached her hands out to touch him at the waist.

He seemed to feel that; he pulled back some, till they were standing more space apart.

"I like it," he said. "It makes things lighter. It makes me feel good."

"It looks just like yellow painted up there," she said. "It looks like something from another world—from the cartoon world." She laughed and kept her teeth showing, afterward, biting on her lower lip. Her front teeth stuck out, anyway, giving a slight curve to her upper lip, like a little breeze there.

"A cartoon," he said. "Things are moving in that direction, since this morning. What about all these rat-faces around and the colored-up air and trees. That's really a cartoon, a whole town—"

"It's Pied Piper Day. It's a day for it. Here in Cuba."

Her voice was light and cool, with just a little tearing in it. "It's just a day once a year in the summer—I forget why—but usually it's a pretty normal town. I was born here. And raised," she said, and she looked down at the ground.

"Yeah," said Billy-Billy. He looked to where the black man had been, but he was turned away now, and sitting, doing something with the other man, their hands down near the grass.

They stood in a silence then, looking at, and away from, each other. Their feet were pointing at each other. Billy-Billy kept turning his neck around like it hurt, but kept coming back to the girl's face, and to her eyes.

She glowed. From the first, he saw how she glowed.

After she left the sidewalk, he had seen where she'd been by the little pieces of light he still could see, where she'd sat down. There was a flicker now near her mouth and coming from behind her head. He wanted to put his face, or his hands, up to her mouth, to get close, maybe against her cheek, and put his arms around her and feel her. He raised one hand slowly up toward her.

"You look nice," he said. "I saw you earlier, on the sidewalk. You look nice."

He felt the words in his mouth.

She said, "I don't know, though. I don't really know."

Looking down, she saw her feet had moved in toward each other, pointing in, so she straightened them out some. She looked back at him, she wanted his face to break into its lines.

"Are you going anywhere now?"

She knew he wasn't.

"No, not really. Yes, and no. I have to go somewhere."

"Can I walk with you for a ways?"

"Sure. You can. Sure, I want you to."

Billy-Billy lifted his bag in one hand, with the rat-mask in it Teddi had left for him to find.

"Let's walk around the block," she said. "It's a wide circle, sort of. By the time we get back to here, to this point, we'll know each other better."

So they did. They walked around the circle. There were a few houses out at this edge of town, and they were silent, hearing only their feet. There were gaps, and vacant lots, and wider fields.

Teddianne wore a white, loose shirt without any buttons, and a pair of light red shorts. She wore socks with tennis shoes. Her head moved along Billy-Billy's shoulder. Billy-Billy paid for her to have a red Popsicle to eat. It made her lips bright-colored.

"We could walk to the horizon if we wanted to," Billy-Billy said.

"Yeah, we could," Teddianne said, looking at her feet on a crack in the sidewalk.

They did the circle again, and again.

Teddianne had another one, a yellow Popsicle. The colors got mixed up on her mouth. The sun started going down, and the moon became barely visible, as they walked, even in the late afternoon.

He was amazed over her. He felt like she was close, like his skin. She was made on, put on to his body. He wanted to stay with her, to sit down and be with her, all night. He had nowhere to go. Already he missed her.

"I was thinking about last night. I was still there. But it was good knowing I was leaving. I took a long shower in hot water. I thought about Ned a lot last night. Then I had bad dreams. I woke up from these dark, close, hot faces. I searched in my mind for the names of God, to bring in light, and it was hard, real hard to find one, any names. But I did. I wanted to say *Father*, then *Almighty Father*, and when I did, I got a sharp, bad pain in my heart. There was a terrible smell, things were resisting me saying that name. I felt like long things were lying down on top of me. But it's like that a lot in there, but not usually that bad."

They walked by where the black men had been, but were now gone. The red sign was brighter, and had a hum.

"I'm scared of things—the past—ever since I was a kid, since Ned, I guess."

"And your grandmother?"

"Yeah. That did something."

Now it was getting dark out. They had been together for hours.

He grazed her hand with the back of his. He saw her white blouse stand out slightly in back where it hung down over her spine.

They sat down on a bus-stop bench, painted orange. They had sat there before, for a little while. The yellow dog Billy-Billy had first seen in town came walking near them. He had cuts on him. He swaggered. He made Billy-Billy, and then Teddi, feel alone, just to see him.

She said, "I know where you can go, tonight, for a while, maybe for a long time, to live. It's around here. It's a place I know about—a lot of people know about it—they don't go there. It's a ways out of town, but you could get there walking, pretty fast. I can show you most of the way."

Billy-Billy had his head down, almost at his knees, resting in his hands. She watched him there in his shape. "What's wrong?" she asked.

Speaking at the ground, he said, "Nothing. Teddianne. I like that name. I like you a lot. When I close my eyes it's like a cyclone. Maybe it was a quick day. Maybe the sun will go all the way down fast and it will be over. It'll be starting again, though, too soon."

Teddianne put a thin white hand on the back of his neck. If he could've seen it.

"Teddianne," he said. "I don't know. Where's this place?"

He raised his head and looked at her. It was like someone

had broken her egg-eyes, and the blue had been spilled out some. She just looked back at him there, on the orange bench, with her hand still on his neck. He had his yellow hat and her torn mask in the bag by his feet.

He said to her, "I like your yellow hair."

"I know you do. I'll take you there—it's called Secret Town Road."

THE PLACE

She took me to the place. It got dark before we got there. Once, I held her hand as we walked, so thin, in mine. I held it so her fingers bunched together. We walked down two dirt roads to get there. She asked me if I'd rather sleep in town at a hotel or somewhere. I told her no.

I said to her, "I like the sound of this place. I'll hear myself walking and moving around out there, alone. Thinking will be easier without the noise. It's been a long time since I slept like that. I like it that only you know where I am. Where I'll be. No one in the world, not anyone, knows where I am now except you."

I was afraid Teddianne wouldn't like me, because of the way I talked. Then I'd sometimes hear the little bird in it.

Teddianne told me her name when we walked around the block. The town square was down a ways and I could see the courthouse peak, a tower with a clock. I was looking at it; there were still some of the leftover colors in the air. The parade was over. She said, "My name's Teddianne. What's yours?"

I said my name. I heard my name inside first; I heard

it that way: "Billy-Billy Jump. They sound the same," I told her. "Our names."

I remembered noticing her walking along across the street and then sitting down. I told her she'd looked like she glowed. I imagined how it felt for her to sit so light on the sidewalk, her being so white and thin and good. I thought that if I stood up close to her and she held her arms down by her sides, or crossed over her chest, no one could see any part of her, from behind me, or maybe from anywhere, if she stood real close. Except they might be able to see the light from her sticking out over my head.

I liked her small bigness. She was a mountain. I wanted to hide her by getting up that close. She was smarter than me, but I thought soon I would be able to be like I was before, when I was younger, more like how I was as a child. Then I felt bright. Things were more perfect how I saw them, even things like the ground, or a broken wheel, or something lying on a chair quiet.

Everything looked like Teddianne did to me now. Things usually looked in-fragments. Once I was watching and seeing my door; I stared at it because it was there. I watched it and it began to make me happier than before, and glad just that it was. It was the moment. Then the knob began to turn. My eyes clouded up with tears. I knew, I thought, it would be Ned coming in to see me, but he was dead by then and the thing stopped after a half turn. But even so, I know, and I knew then, that it was him all the time. Now I thought that it could have been Teddianne coming in. That would be okay, and I put it in my memory. Putting that in there like that made all the rest of the thoughts I'd had since then better, prettier-mind.

She took me to a hill bank where an overgrown path led downhill. There was a single, still-lit street lamp down at the bottom, off to one side. She stopped and stretched back away from me. She had taken my hand. Her arm looked like a long pole-thing in the dark. I could still see her face, and her eyes looked half-closed.

"I have to go back now," she said. "I don't really want to—but I have to. I got to go see Eddie. He's old and I help him lock up, to get ready for the night."

I felt something in my chest and my hands went damp. I let go of her hand but for the fingers. I didn't know if I'd ever see her again. I saw myself alone, on this secret road, with the knife, two thin things, it and me.

"Teddianne," I said. "Can I just go in one of these houses and sleep? Can I come see you at Eddie's tomorrow?"

"Yeah, you can," she said. "No one comes out here anymore. They've just forgotten, it seems. Most people don't like to think about it, I guess—because of what was done to the people there. Eddie can tell you better—but it's safe. You can be in any of them."

I let her go. She had a walk back to town. It seemed strange, and wrong, to see her slip away, thin, just sliced into the darkness, but then that's what she did. That's just what she did. I wanted to run after her, and put my hands on her, one on the back and one on her stomach, even with each other at the same time and holding in. But I didn't.

At a distance, when I was cutting down the bank, I heard her give me a whistle. Two notes. One low, and one high, like a bird. Like her. It was from her face, to me. I listened again, then whistled it back the same way, but there was only the silence in its blackness to me.

Down on the other, lower dirt road, I walked toward and past the street lamp. It must have shined there for years. I touched the wooden pole. I stood under its light. Then I moved away from it, and went walking on down what Teddianne called Secret Town Road.

I got to the row of houses. They were old. They looked alike in the way they stood. They were very quiet standing. They looked out at the road. They had faces. Some seemed more awake than others. There was a small brown-looking house in the dark. It had a screen porch. Some had open front porches with the porch floor even with the ground, without any steps at all. The ground came right up to them.

I walked past some of them, looking into their doors and windows from the road's edge. I went until I picked a white house with a flat porch with a water pump on the porch's side. It didn't look that bad, or that old, just deserted. The windows were broken. I went in by the front screened door. The main door was gone. Inside, it was dark. Darker light, from somewhere, was coming in the broken windows, and through the screened door.

I pushed around with my feet on the wood floor. There was glass, and what felt like cans, or vases, and short wooden legs from a bed or a child's table. I knew I'd made a mistake to come here. I thought of Teddianne walking home toward real light.

I went over to the window and watched out. I looked at the quiet road. All the front yards were connected. There was a dusty smell. I haunched down on the glass chips, in the corner, at its V. I saw the room grow some lighter; I felt aware some, of all the life there had been before in this, in all these houses. Now it was just me here alone. I leaned my head against a wall and closed my eyes. When I did, I felt a stirring in the house. I heard the flapping of many wings. I heard them in the back room, flying out the back windows. Some hit against the ceilings. My mind went cold; I cowered down into my knees. I couldn't believe I was there.

I'd seen a flock of white-winged birds flying overhead earlier, when I was walking with Teddianne. Their wings underneath showed a flashing white, all of them linked together in the air. I'd looked at Teddianne and she had white coming from her, too. "Who are you?" I asked her. "Who have I met?" When I asked her, she just cocked her head back, and with her lips pressed together more than usual; she looked back at me, and she let it go, she let go of her light and came into my mind—it got in behind my face and settled down into me. Thinking of that now took away the cold and the bats. I slipped down and sat still in the corner of the room. "Teddianne," I said. "Teddianne."

There was nothing else to do now but try to sleep. In my bag I had a rolled-up blanket. I got it out of the prison. They let me have it. I took the two deers out and put them on the floor near where my face would be. I folded the blanket in two and got in between. I slept fast, my head on my bag for a pillow. I dreamt of my father and his hands. They shook; they reached out to me but never got there, but they shook a different color than I'd ever seen hands before. He looked sick, or scared, and later I cried in the dream; I could feel it in my throat.

Then I dreamt of *her*. It had been a long time. She was different now. She had changed bodies. She was talking and gesturing with her hands, waving, cutting the air. I was behind her. I waited, I felt unhappy waiting, but when she turned I saw her face. It was bright-lighted yellow. Then her hands kept talking, making a loud flapping sound. It woke me. It was the bats. They were back and they flew near my face. I felt other things in the room, long presences. My father and the yellow girl faded and were there invisible. But the bats were real. I reached in my bag and put on my hat to protect my head, so they wouldn't get in my hair. I put on the broken rat-mask to hide my face. I wrapped up in them, blanket to my chin.

It was hot. I lay there disguised, hidden, and wrapped inside an abandoned house where I felt people had been tormented, and where my father's hands shook in fear, of me. And I had seen *her* again. She was here with me, too, crushing the broken glass in the corner in the shadows with a yellow light.

"Teddianne," I thought.

PALE LIGHT

I felt fevered on the floor. I was grinning behind the rat-mask. In my mask and hat, I lay there and drifted into sleep.

Half-asleep I had a dream vision of Teddianne cutting through the houses at Secret Town. I opened my eyes to see out the eye holes in my mask. I saw Teddi lighting matches at the windows, looking in.

She saw me. Then she was up to me, kneeling down. She lit a last match and held it high above her head and the light shone down on us. She whispered something, she put a finger to her lips. Then she laughed, at my looks. I made room for her in my blanket. Then she stood up and took off first her shoes, then her pants. I saw her naked from behind her. She was a pale light of the room. I reached out and touched her behind her knee.

When she got in with me, she lay with her face to me, up to mine. My hand touched her backside. She spoke to me, close. She said, "I'd take my shirt off too, but my breasts aren't very big at all." She leaned in closer against me. I saw my face break into a thousand lines.

SOURCE

In the dawn, I thought of the road out front as a creek. I would've gone to jump in, to bathe. I could go out and lie down in the red road; I might feel its tug, because it was a motion in itself. I got up and looked out the window at it. There was a ditch alongside its other side, with little flowers growing by it, little smells. I brought the petals up close to my face. I could wrap one around my whole face, I made it so big, so thin and almost transparent, like it had tiny, many tiny veins of smell running through it.

It was early, still wet out. Too early to see Teddianne yet. I could go anyway and watch her house and wait to see it moving, alive with the daytime come. But, kneeling over, rolling up my blanket, I thought to roll it back out. I sat back on my blanket. It had been with me too, all night long. I had carried it to this place, and into this town and in the black truck, and from the road, and first from the outside door from the prison place, and before, inside there, waiting. It was mine. I sat on it against the wall of the broken-up house. It was still fairly dark inside, totally private compared to where I had been only yesterday.

I closed my eyes.

"Teddianne," I thought. I opened my eyes and looked at a broken window, broken in a circle, like a web in a spiral. I shifted my view to the opposite corner, to the other V, and closed my eyes again. I did nothing, but let go. It got to where there were great moments of good, when the thoughts came rarely. When they did they felt good, like they were being pulled through me on a sweet chain. In between the thoughts was the best place I'd ever been; just silent, packed feeling, but quiet, like everything was waiting to be good all around myself. All the things I ever liked were in there, imbedded in the quiet, tiny. Then the yellow started coming. First the yellow color like the hat, then a yellow, lighter, hair color, then a yellow feeling. There were hundreds of yellows. They led up to my throat. I put back my head and opened my mouth to let some out. Then I saw how yellows weren't yellow at all, but were made out of no-color, then only later they changed to become their colorness, yellow. Thousands of yellows. I put my tongue to them all to taste them.

I got up and took my bag and my blanket with me. I wore the hat in the morning sun. I went by the still-lit lamp, touching it again, and up the path on the short bank. Then I stood where Teddianne had left me. I looked the way she must've gone. I followed, in that direction, into town. I found traces of the Pied Piper along the way. Crepe-paper ribbons caught on the trees. The paper lanterns were still hung. But it felt more normal. The town's breath was more regular than yesterday's. It led me to the street where Teddianne lived.

It was too early to see her. I thought of her sleeping, her face closed, and then how it might look, sleepy, when she did open her eyes.

I thought that when you're tired you want to close your eyes, but when you're dead you have to close your eyes. I wandered over a couple of houses to the alley that ran between. I went and sat against a dark woodshed, my back to it, and waited for the sun to heat the day up, to dry things so I could get over to her.

I watched my feet. I held my legs with my hands locked together below my knees. I felt my mouth fall into a familiar shape, of when I am sitting, quiet, serious. I felt very quiet, again. What I looked at felt like a part of me.

When I went back to the house, Teddi was inside the front door, yelling at a man she called Harry. I pushed in through the screen door with the "Little Miss Sunbeam" sign on it in a metal plate. She didn't see me come in. I went down a short aisle and listened to her.

"I know, Harry, I know you have been."

Teddianne was yelling in an old man's ear, big, like a flap of fried dough, that couldn't probably hear anymore.

"It's like a war, isn't it, Harry? Like Fredericksburg, right?"

Harry shook his head up and down.

"Yep. It been ten days they ain't come yet. How am I supposed to eat without them?"

"Harry, Eddie won't let you starve. You've got credit," she yelled.

"I'll get some sardines," he said, "and a can of ravioli, too. Ten days and no money to eat."

"Teddianne," I said so she couldn't hear it. But she turned like she had. She didn't see me through the cans on the shelf. I stood behind them. I looked at Harry's ears. I saw a man, a person who had lived a long time, had done so

many things. It was all with him. No one could see it or know
it all, but everything Harry'd done was on him, in him somewhere. Little impressions, like spoon-pushed onto him, and
big ones slammed into his body, all packed into his insides.
Maybe when he was worn out from carrying them all around
was when he'd die. There were lines all over his face, and
in his ears, like the bands, the circles in a cut tree. It was
all there in a code, on him. It made him look the way he
did, and act like he did.

I thought, "He fills up the whole place." I just filled up
this small area because I was younger. I thought about all
that people had done, over the years. It was too much. I saw
Teddianne over there, taking up a little space, cooling it,
and Eddie who was old, too, filled up the whole house and
the corner lot, too. "Our brains have lines on them from what
we do," I thought. Probably born smooth and then the ditches
begin.

Teddianne was different here. She looked older. Her
hands flashed when she talked with them to the old man.
There were dark lines under her eyes. There was blue color
on her neck and at her temples, fine, where the veins ran
through. Her hair was flyaway. I imagined my fingers around
her upper arms like bracelets.

"Teddianne."

"Hey," she said when she saw me. "It's you."

We had yesterday between us. Harry gave me a look,
like a baby. He had to squint some after he first saw me. I
was very near to the cans on the shelf. He might have gotten
me confused with them. They were green-wrapped paper on
metal, ribbed, and some red, and blue, and with pictures.

There I was. Harry looked back at Teddianne, then moved on to the kitchen and to Eddie.

"How was it?" she asked.

When she talked, her voice drifted into her hands.

"It was okay. It was interesting. I feel like I'm still out there in a way. I was lucky to find it, I guess. I mean, you knew about it. Lucky to find you, I mean."

"You can put down your bag, back here if you want to."

"Okay, maybe later," I said. I stood there holding my things. It was too light out, in the world. "So this is where you work," I said. "You live here, too?"

"Yes, I do," she said.

Then I didn't have anything more to say to her. I watched her neck to see where it could've been broken, or slanted. It looked straight.

"You okay?" she asked.

She had moved to behind the pay counter, with it between us.

"I'm just funny today," I said. "Everything's coming new, is all. I guess last night was pretty funny, too. Thought of you, out there. I mean, not too much. Am I keeping you?" There was no one in the old store but the dust, and then us, and the old men cracking in the back.

I reached up for my hat, to hold it. It was in the bag in my hand. Teddianne's mask was, too.

"Look," she said.

She lifted up her shirt.

On her stomach was a bright-colored circle. It was a tattoo, in reds and blue, made like a thin, spinning wheel. There was yellow on the inside edge of it, coating it, making the other color stay brighter. It was on her skin. Right on her body.

"Whewww," I let out the air.

"It's more me than anything else," she said. "I don't look like I should since the wreck, but this is always the same, always bright."

We stood there for a while. The sun was shining through.

"I got a tattoo, too," I told her, "only mine is inside. I found out about it from an X-ray when I was a boy. I had a pain in my chest, so they looked inside, and found it. A hole. There were two hole scars on the inside of my chest and my back. They were even with each other."

"So there were round marks in you? Still there?"

"Yeah. They're still there. But not in color like yours. Maybe red. But they're marks—tattoos; they're inside. They have to do with you, like yours."

Teddianne watched me close. She looked at me. Right at me, in my eyes. I felt the marks connected to how she was looking at me.

Some women with children with them were watching us now. They had groceries in their arms where the kids usually went. One tugged at one woman's dress. The other one just had big eyes. Teddianne rang up the food and put it into bags for them. She flinched sometimes, just her face, but sometimes she jerked her fingers back from the register keys. Later, she told me there was a short and if she did a certain thing wrong, then she got a shock. But I thought she was flinching from her feelings about me, about the things we'd talked about. I thought she would always flinch from having feelings inside her heart that were connected to her face, that I liked so much. She seemed so tender, and her blue eyes in her face, looking out at the world. I wanted to get back there behind them.

While she worked I wandered back to the doorway that led to the kitchen. It was off the grocery part of the house. All it had was an old stove and a big sink in it. There was other stuff, but that was all the kitchen things it had, and the small carved-on wooden table where Harry and Eddie were sitting at the coffee.

I didn't go deep into the room. I leaned on the doorjamb, it was blue, and listened to Harry and Eddie talk. I could hear the sound they made when they put their cups down into the saucers, a throaty, glassy sound.

"It was the Jackson boy that done it. With a BB gun," Harry said. "He kept the police off with it, with a toy gun. Not like mine. It's real. It's a replica, but it shoots."

"It used to shoot. It's old now, it may not even cock itself anymore."

Eddie was the younger of the two men. He had poems he wrote pasted to the refrigerator door. I could see one of them, its title. It said, "Nature Boy."

"Never did cock itself, never did that, anyway," answered Harry.

"Used to come in here carrying a hatchet and a hunting knife—and picked fights. He's a wild boy, crazy, that's for sure. I pulled his daddy out of the creek once. Thought he was drowning himself. But he was just swimming. Damn fool didn't tell me that till I'd drugged him clear out and up to the bank. Should of seen the look on his face."

Both the old men had a laugh.

"But I run him out of here many a time. Threw his motorbike over on its side in the alley one time. Of course that was ten years ago, when the bar was running. Before my fingers got so curled up."

"He owes me for a brand-new bath towel, he does. Put it on the electric heater and it burnt up. Busted a lamp shade, too."

THE HOUSE

I lived at Secret Town Road. No one but her knew where I was, unless someone followed me out there. I didn't make many trips. Maybe some boys saw me in the woods, but I never knew.

I waited for Teddianne to come, but she didn't.

I walked down the edges of the clay road by myself. I didn't want to walk right in the road. I imagined myself right in the middle of the road but couldn't make myself do it for long.

I missed how she made me feel. I went out and stood by the trees, and looked away, then went that direction and stood in other places. I sat in the tall, brown grass in the thin woods near the street of abandoned houses.

I dreamt of different people at night. I wore the hat, but not the mask. I was in another room. I dreamt of women, and only felt half-awake. I dreamt of seeing ghosts in the houses, all of them but mine, then realized I was the ghost in this house. I dreamt of a woman without a head, and there were people with real rat-faces, not just masks, and then her head was Suzanne's, then Teddianne's.

It rained on the road in front of the house. Normally, the road was orange-colored, now it got sticky with red mud holes, and pockets. I stayed in the house.

Teddianne.

I stayed in the corner touching the two walls with my back.

GIRL

Then, in town, I saw her again. She was in a window. She saw me first. I looked at my shadow. Then that lonely time started to be over. We talked on the steps of the brick library, and she told me she waited for me to come. She looked thin and small. She said to me that when she was really young she could fly, and had once in the front yard.

She took me to the old house where she lived. I met Eddie. I had coffee between him and Harry and Teddianne. The table was too small for all of us, so she sat away from it, her hands resting on her knees.

She was beautiful. She was there under the painting of a horse head, near where Eddie had old clothes and coats hanging down from a long silver bar. The wiring was exposed up on the wall by a fan, and most of the room was filled with wooden cases of old Coke bottles. The heat in the wintertime was the stove top with a fan to blow the heat onto Eddie.

The house was very close to the house next door, and had a bright green strip of grass running between. I would look out of Teddianne's window, resting my head, looking down at that strip of green. I could hear the people in the other house, yelling.

It was an interesting town. I was glad being there, with her, and those that came through, near that green. At night, we talked and I walked home many nights to the secret house that was mine.

One night, when Teddianne was gone, I had a long talk with Eddie. He had a cracking voice in the kitchen. He talked about Teddianne, and about Secret Town.

"I heard she flew in the air," I told him.

"God, I don't know about anybody flying. I heard it too, of course. I don't think anyone believed it, though, not even them that say they saw it. Her father. He's over his hill now. He pushed those two girls. Sandy—well, she's gone away with some boy. Had a baby that died. An awful thing. Yeah, there's lots of rumors about them two. Always was. Teddi was always the brightest girl in this town. She stayed to herself a long time, then when she came out—she flew, all right, she flew with a wild group for a while, then she had a bad accident, she'll tell you all about it. It knocked her down a long time. Then she came here. She used to come down here when she was little, with her brother, and she'd take her seat on top of that pop cooler, same spot every day. Couple of boys killed in that wreck she was in. She looks a little different, but mostly it's in here," he said, and he pointed.

"Her head?"

"She ain't crazy. Just changed. Complains about it, about not seeing right, or being right, or something. I don't know. But I do know—she's got a power, she's definitely got a power."

He stopped talking a while to light a cigarette. He opened a bottle of beer. With his gnarled-up hands it took a while, and I watched him, wanting to help, scared to offer, scared of him too, but I wanted to know him. It's what he knew, his marks and his depth, that scared me.

LIKE A
CHILD

I had my statue of the two deer out on a windowsill near where I slept. The whole house was cleaner now and better. It seemed no one in the real town knew anything about me, or Teddianne, or Eddie even. And they never came out to my road. It didn't look like it connected to other roads.

I named the deer statue "Teddianne," but I never said it out loud right to it, only just in my mind.

The first time she invited me to her room, she was nervous. She said, "I just live upstairs. I got a lot of pictures of people, and books and things. You don't have to come up if you don't want to. No one's ever been up there, except Eddie, of course. And once, Sandy, a long time ago—last summer when she was here in town. Come on." She yelled, "Eddie, I'm going up."

I watched her back pockets up the stairs. We walked down a mushy hallway to her room at the end.

"This is it," she said.

She nodded at a picture on the wall.

"There's Stonewall Jackson. He's my favorite."

Then she pointed at the picture framed on the little table she had.

"Robert E. Lee, of course. He was great, too," she said.

I sat on the bed. There were no chairs in the slanted room.

"I was born in South America," she said.

"Really?" I watched her loom up at me, then get back to normal size.

"Well, no, not really. I was born in Cuba, actually."

She kneeled down on her floor in front of me, playing with her hands while I watched her.

"What's that map there?" I said.

"It's sort of a hobby of mine," she said. "I think about the war, those battles. And the people that lived there. I guess they were people."

"You're beautiful, Teddianne, so beautiful," I told her.

"I used to get bloody noses," she said. "I was always getting hit in the nose a lot. That's why it's funny-looking now."

I said, "You look good. You don't have to say those things to me."

"I was okay before the accident I had. It messed up my face, like you see it. It made me forget things, though, I think. That's what bothers me most about it. I think I forgot who I really am."

I put my hands on her head. From in between my hands, her face in the middle, she said to me, "I flew, in the air. For real. A light came out of my head through my eyes. I saw everything golden. I was swinging on a swing—my brother put it up there, high in the tree. It broke while I was on it.

I stayed in the air, by myself, for a little while. It was the best feeling I ever had. I held myself there. I spread out all around the yard, and the house, the whole neighborhood. My dad was smoking a cigarette. I remember the smoke from it. My sister was there, too, watching. Even my mom was there. That seems like the last time we were together, all of us. Later, a few weeks later, I got in a car with a boy, and we got hit. After that, I stopped feeling like a kid. We got hit really bad, and some other boys died."

She reached over; we were on the floor. She squeezed my hand. She put her face to mine. She kissed me on the mouth, pushing hers on me. She kissed me like a child. She tasted that way. She kissed me with her lips open, and her eyes were closed inside her.

Teddianne kissed me for a long time. The light changed in the room.

She let go. She moved back a little ways. I felt her mouth breathing. She was propped up by her arm, her hand to the floor. She moved her lips but didn't speak.

Then she said, "My dead brother, Charles, visited me once. It was the night Sandy's baby died. My sister's baby. He was deformed. He died after only a few days. The whole town knew about her. That night I got into bed with her. She didn't have a man to be with. Not really. She wouldn't let me hold her. I lay there in the dark and looked at the back of her head, and felt how much I loved her. I cried for her, and for me. We were so far apart then. I watched her in the darkness, her shape. I could see those little dots in the air. I looked over to the other bed and saw Charles lying there watching Sandy from her front side. He was crying, too. He looked at me. He had different-colored hair, but it was him.

He had the same two teeth missing that made a long, dark hole the longer I looked at it. I looked there a long time. He was gone in the morning. Now you're Charles. To me. You're Sandy, too, in a way—how it used to be. You're my dad, too. I love you."

Her words were like a lot of pretty glass in her mouth.

I thought of the children inside her, the thousands of children she had been, day to day, growing up. I wanted to see each face and hear each of her voices. I leaned and kissed her mouth that said those things. Teddianne. I loved her there. I kissed each lip, each part of her mouth by itself. I held her. She was small behind my hands. I was out of breath wanting her, and having her, and hearing her. I got close with her on the floor. Teddianne. I saw her put her neck back, where the muscles could be seen. There was a hollow at her throat. Her fingers touched her shirt-front buttons. She was naked underneath. Her nails were shiny, her fingers touched together against themselves. I held her under her arms against her side-chest, where it was hot.

My hands went down her back, along her spine. Her hips were small to hold. That's when she got me, and I never let go.

Teddianne. I got inside her. I felt the rest of me coming in. My hands were behind her neck, holding her head, her face, so close. I put my hands down below her and pulled, lifted her into me. She raised her knees up, to alongside of me. I never forgot that, when she did that.

"You hit the end of me, inside," she said.

"Me too," I said.

I held her shoulders like straps, my palms holding where it was rounded. When I touched the stop inside her, I saw the white light. Her teeth, she was born with them, she said. I licked them; her words came out and stuck on their white and stayed on her red lips.

She said, "Billy-Billy, you're everybody now. Get in me again," she said. "The stop place. I remember it now."

LIPSTICK

We spent many days and nights in Teddi's room, moving toward late summer together. We didn't leave Eddie's house very much. Sometimes I went to Secret Town, just be there in the daytime, to sit on a front porch alone, and watch the dirt road and the trees. I listened for the small noises. I could hear a twig break out there.

Summer was a hot blanket we got under. It rained and the street would heat up the water. Teddianne made a mud dam at the bottom of a black street. I watched her sit in the brown water. We walked at night, quiet on the cooled-down, pebbly sidewalks, big cracks in them where Teddianne stubbed her toe. I pulled back when she touched the blood from her foot to her mouth, to taste it, with her finger. Then she smeared it on her face like lipstick, all over her mouth. She sat on the pavement and stared at me standing back at the edge of the dark.

Sometimes Eddie went out with us, slowly. In the days the dogs panted, and at night we touched, looking for cool areas of the body.

ME AND HER

Teddianne and me, we walked down the alleys, between houses and stores. They were long, and light-filled. At night they were black. We walked down those tunnels together.

The strip between her house and the next one was child-green, green-bright like you dreamed of as a boy or girl. It was thin and ran long. Up above it was the gap, long like it, and filled in with blue sky, or white, or black, star-dotted.

Teddi had hands I got to touch. I liked her. I liked how she looked—from behind her, her inside her pants, when she walked, or stood, or even sat down I liked, her hips seen from the front view, spread out to sit, to hold her. Naked, she was still skinny pale, so sweet to me. So long, kissing, and licking, and tasting. It was dear. We were, we were like older babies, tasting, and sucking, and up close, wet-faced, and without any minds at all. Her fingers, her cheeks, her lips: her eyes were the blue, and up close mine blurred, crossed some and saw only her color. Her stomach, her neck, her tongue. Teddianne.

YELLOW

One night I put on the yellow paint for Billy-Billy. I bought it at a store. It was children's paint. I bent over it, squatted down beside the can of it. I poured it into a blue bucket Eddie had. I stirred it with a wooden spoon. Currents moved in it with a lapping, a gurgling sound. Billy-Billy told me about the little prison bird and about how his insides had been touched by it, when it sang. There had been his yellow hat now left out at Secret Town.

I touched the surface of the paint, its face, with my fingertip. I pulled it out, dripping. I stuck it into my mouth. The paint can had said it wasn't a poison; it was made for children. I sucked the yellow color. I put some down on me, between my legs. I put a lot down there. I put the paint on my face, just some, and then all over my mouth. It tasted yellow. It dripped out of my mouth and on my lips and down my chin. I was naked. Billy-Billy was sleeping. Dear Billy-Billy, dear Billy-Billy.

I went in, quietly, and pulled the covers down. He sleeps with a sheet over us. He moved a little; he was on his back. I kissed him. I put my face down on him and slid it lightly.

I went down to him there; I put him in my mouth and started to forget everything but that. I sucked, so yellow and warm, slick paint, it was grainy some, too. I sucked on him so yellow.

Then I got up and turned on the light so he could see me. I was never happier, never. I lost a sense of my body, in a way. I felt my face on, and I asked him, please, please, to come and get me. Come and get me, get me close. I got down on the floor on my face, and put my knees on the ground, too. I stuck straight up, backside at him.

"Billy-Billy, get inside of me, please. Get as deep in me as you ever can and stay in me for a whole night and day."

He got in me. He said, "Teddianne." He said, "You're so little. You're so beautiful." He said to me, "Teddianne."

He got in me for two hours and twenty minutes because that was one-tenth of a day, and also a part of a whole year, a part of the earth turning once, and we turned that way together. Oh, God, he got into me so deep and my yellow face just pushed on the floor and I pushed back at him and I felt his spirit, his soul, come into me and begin to live there, like he wanted to. I saw, I tasted white, I was flying from top of a tall tree in the wind, that made my face change, and even different colors in that air. It was so much, so terrible, so God, Jesus, come back!

KISS

It was September when I stood on Teddi's bed, watching down on her under just halfway, a sheet, her mouth painted yellow, and me, painted down there, and some on my mouth yellow, too.

I told Teddianne that we could go out and let people see her and me.

"When will we go?" she said.

"Any minute," I said. "Can we drive Eddie's car? Will he have to come with us?"

"I don't know if he can come or not. I wish he could in a way, but in another way I know we have to go alone," and we planned on going home. Moving in ourselves to where I had been, I was taking Teddianne with me there. There were cornfields and flat, dark ground, and nighttime there she would look good in.

She put on a dress that was black, and a belt with silver punch holes to tighten it. She wore it loose and slung down and then tight as it could go at the waist. She put her hands both up to the mirror, pressed flat to it, and looked close at her face in between them. I watched from close behind her.

She looked good in that black dress. Her feet were together. She leaned forward and kissed the mirror, her hands holding, her long fingers bending on, the glass beside her face. She kissed her own mouth, her own face, in the mirror for a long time. Her eyes closed slowly and she tilted her head to the side. Her hands stayed flat by her head. On the mirror her fingers curled. She kissed herself, her lips pushing hard. She pushed and she kissed there. Her mouth slid down and wetness built up on the mirror from her mouth and where she breathed through her nose.

SMALL
WHITE

We were going down a winding, curved gray road. We had Eddie's car for the trip. It was three hundred miles to where I'd lived before with those people, with Suzanne, and with me.

Teddi's eyes changed shapes. Changed. She turned in the seat and held her back to me; she watched the road out the window. "I like looking out the window," she said. She pulled up her shirt and I saw her bare back. "Me and Eddie used to drive to Laurel and back, but not too often. He has a sister there. He got stuff for the store there, from a guy." She turned around in the seat and faced right at me. She was holding her shirt up with both hands.

"Here," she said. "See?"

We told Eddie about the trip, standing in the kitchen one night before he went upstairs, but he said, "Goddammit, why you got to run off everywhere? I've been everywhere. They used to know me everywhere. Eddie Parker; they knew me up in Chicago, New York. I lived there, years ago. Goddammit, it's the same old shit everywhere. Might as well just stay here where you belong."

I saw Teddianne stand there, at him. She leaned closer and put her thin arm out to him. The two of them together; he was bent from old age, his arms were thin with thick blue veins. He wore sandals on his feet. Both of them were bent. They knew each other's eyes.

"I want you to come back, Teddianne. You have to come back. How am I going to get around without the car?" He raised his eyebrows at her.

We laughed with him, he and the voice, the sound of the old sage.

Teddianne said, "Eddie, Billy-Billy'll drive. We'll be back."

"Billy-Billy? He ain't got no driver's license. He was in prison. Billy-Billy ain't got no driving rights."

"I used to have a license," I said, "but it expired."

She was always wearing those small white shirts that were too short, and she'd have it maybe unbuttoned one at the bottom. When she said that about driving, she raised both her arms up in the air and rested them on her head and her shirt came up and there was her stomach and I could see the tattoo.

I could never be without her anymore. In the beginning I could have, out at Secret Town, but not now, not since she painted me yellow.

Eddie said, "Hell, I don't have any driving license, either." His big forearms were like a cartoon man's.

On the highway when we passed dead animals I always got a chill through me. Even if I waited awhile, it'd sneak through me and be cold. It was getting dark. People were turning on their house lights alongside the narrow highway. It felt good to drive a car again. The air coming in the windows made me glad Teddianne was with me.

We passed a little girl who looked like a small Teddianne to me. She waved and I watched her in the rearview disappear down the road. But I knew she was still there, even after she was over the back hill, out of sight.

PICTURE

Then I remembered a time with Suzanne.

I sat her up on a table once, at her house, up on the countertop in the kitchen. She wore a dress with a pink-colored shirt on top. She sat up on the counter with her back to the cabinets, and she opened up her legs to me. She just parted them and put her feet out to the sides as far as she could. Her ankles hung down off the edge of the counter, and then I knew, I knew about girls, about their way, women, and how they opened up. They had to open up to you with their bodies *and* with their feelings—their hearts. Men could just get in, not opened up that much sometimes, it seemed, but Suzanne opening up that much like that, and her legs just opening for me, up there on the kitchen counter, with a dress on, and the look on her face, showed me that.

"Let's stop," said Teddianne. "Can't we stop for a while and do something? Have some fun, or something? I don't want to get there too fast, do you?"

She had packed a suitcase and it rode now in the back seat of the car. She put her clothes and things, but not many, in it. It was so light when I carried it out. I just brought a few things with me in a bag. We drove off in the afternoon, the day after talking to Eddie about it. We had driven around some the night before to get used to the feel and the idea of it. Just drove around the town and a little ways out of it. I knew I was living loose, moving through the summer and now fall with her, riding now, putting my clothes in a bag, but I felt young still and that a lot of things would happen to me over a long, long time.

"Yeah, let's do. Let's pull in and get a drink, and eat something—or somebody."

We drove on till we saw a place. We were in a fairly large little town, stuck on the end of the two-lane where it spread out, letting us inside. It was dark out.

"Sometimes I feel like a drink," she said. "Sometimes it's good."

"I know," I told her.

I looked back at the blue car we left across the street, waiting for us. Looking in it, it seemed funny that we had fit in it at all. It seemed impossible to fit inside anywhere.

We walked on the street. I held her by the arm, above her elbow.

"I like your face," I told her.

"I know," she said. "I believe you. It's my yellow hair you like."

I nodded to the place we were headed to. She sucked her lips in as we hit the curb.

There were just a few people inside the dark lounge bar.

There were tables and a jukebox, and a dance floor with nobody on it. Teddianne had a beer, then another, and with it a shot of whiskey. Each time she threw down a shot, she would set her glass down and look at me hard in the eye, holding on.

"I'm rough and tough," she said.

I was surprised they served her, but she looked the man in the eye and changed him, forever, I thought. He'd do whatever she asked of him. As I had a drink, I felt the hard walls of my head soften.

"Those shots are bigger than your head," I said.

The dance floor started to take on a meaning. A small short-haired girl came out dressed in a little body suit zipped up to her throat, cut in close with no sleeves to it. She was a stripper and I watched her getting ready for the show. Music came up, people turned to see.

Teddianne said, "I know her. I knew her since I was in fourth grade. She's Gail. She was my friend. Now look at her. I wish we could take her home, or somewhere—with us."

Gail was sliding her zipper down.

"Maybe she likes dancing," I said.

Gail was peeling her suit back off her shoulders. She had small bony shoulders.

"When I was in fourth grade, Gail used to sit behind me and braid my hair and make me nervous. Now she's making me nervous again," Teddianne said.

"You and her—in grade school together," I said.

"Let's go. Let's get out of here," said Teddianne, making me the sad one in the scene.

• • •

In the car, in the dark, a thunderstorm was starting as we moved on along toward Chamlin again. Teddianne was not hardly talking much at all. Then she said, "I was reading about Iceland."

"Yeah?" I answered.

"Fifty-five percent of the people of Iceland believe in elves. Did you know that?"

"No, I didn't know that," I said.

"Yes, well, maybe you and me—and Eddie—should move there—and Gail."

"You speak Icelandic?" I said.

"Oh, yeah, I forgot," she said.

We were in a big lightning storm now; I saw a dead dog lit up by the side of the road. I hoped Teddianne didn't see it. She was staring straight ahead. Then she thought lightning was hitting the roof of the car. She wanted to pull over. We sat in the flashing light, seeing those big rolled-up bales of grass in the fields, lighting up like daytime.

"Lightning's hitting the car, isn't it?" she said.

"No, it's not hitting the car," I said.

We started up again and passed many things in the dark. I felt it was moving too fast, our time, our lives now. I felt the winds blowing around my head even with the car windows up. Teddianne was changing, in the car, each moment. She danced to the car radio. The rhythm moved her body off the car seat, her hands waving, jerking around, and it could be seen on her face, the jumping around of time. Her head, and her yellow hair, bouncing around. There was something, though, getting at me, a fear. With the dashboard lights on we went through the little white towns that slept. It was a new darkness for us, and Teddianne's and my reflections in the windshield were balloonlike, two faces, sticking up, suspended on the ends of strings.

THE OLD HOUSE

It was too late to go anywhere I knew people. My folks were asleep, my mother, small in her bed. They had two beds. They used to. It was the same house Mama K had lived in, with the stained ceiling, a painted ceiling of childhood times. Her mirror had my puffed-up, cried face in it somewhere, maybe in the attic. His face was on the front of the house.

I wished Teddianne and I could sleep in those two old beds, facing each other in the darkened room with a little light coming through the window. On her face the light would look good.

"Where should we go?" she asked. "Can we go by your house—just to look at it? Can we go in and sleep in it tonight?"

"No, not tonight," I said. "We should've gotten here earlier. But we can't.

"Look"—I pointed—"that's where I went to school. Ned won a red ribbon at something there. Those ribbons were a big thing to us. Ned drank bottles of Coke all day. I remember always seeing him walking toward the Coke machine, and those ribbons. I can see him from the back, how he looked.

He used to look at the bottom of the bottle to see where the bottle was made at—the city is printed there."

I wanted to get out of the car and lie down in the wading pool with Teddianne. It would be empty now; it was a shallow, turquoise-color cement. Just lie there in the night light, our clothes catching most of it in the wrinkles.

"We'll go by my house last. Maybe we can sleep in the car by the house or down by the Home. In the morning my dad would see us and come out. He'd crouch down near us and watch. I think he'd know it was me, even under covers. He'd touch my head, and wake me. He'd talk to me. He might accidentally wake you up first, your yellow head. He'd like that."

We drove on. I knew something was going to happen, something real fast, when it started.

NED'S
HOUSE

That's where Ned lived."

I looked where Billy-Billy pointed. I expected to see a
tiny house made out of uneven boards and painted all red or
green, faded. I thought it'd be on a little piece of ground,
with a little walkway and a knocked-in hole for a crawl door.
Maybe a large statue of Jesus Himself there, standing taller
than a child's house, looking happy.

I thought all that in a quick picture before looking out
the window. I was in Billy-Billy's town. I felt different. I felt
like a different color, inside, and out. I put my hand down
on my circle under my shirt. I could feel where the color part
was and wasn't.

"How could that be Ned's house?" I said. "It's a regular
big house."

"This is big Ned's house. He was a friend of my dad's.
I think they probably named Ned after him."

We passed places from his past. Then I said to him, "Let's
go do it somewhere. Let's go do it on the ground. I want to

feel the ground on my back, with you in me. I want to feel my behind in it. We'd really be in the town then."

We drove to a dirt road where there was the old Masonic Home. He pulled the blue car way over to one side, facing up the hill toward his old house, with its back end to the Home. I got out of the car and left the door open. There wasn't any light in the road to see by. I pulled my shirt over my head. I curled up my fingers for him to come to me. I took off my pants, and my shoes. I stood there in the grass-dirt of his childhood. Standing with my knees together, there was a space open between my thighs. I took off my panties. I let him see my white backside.

The blue car was on a slant.

We got down on the ground. He held my waist and put his hand on my behind. I put my face and front down on the ground. He put his fingers inside of me from behind. I lifted up so that he could get them in.

"Billy-Billy," I said. "Billy-Billy. Billy-Billy Jump." I turned over and let him get inside me from the front.

After a short time, down there near the Home, where Ned was, with the breeze blowing along the road, and the night-blue car, I climbed over the seat back and lay in by Billy-Billy to sleep a few hours before the day came.

HER

We didn't bother to drive the car up the hill in the morning. It was a fresh morning, quiet; there were small colored flowers on the side road, some pressed down where we had lain on them in the night.

We walked up the hill, holding hands. We left everything back in the car, sitting there, slanted. The first thing I thought of when I saw the old house in the morning was the statue of the little deers I'd left at Secret Town. The light had risen and was shining on them, too. It was Mama K's once. I felt aware of her above me, high up, and the deers behind me in a straight line and the house I grew up in, right in front of me. The house felt very quiet. I knew they were in there —they lived quiet lives. Their car sat out in front of the house.

I knocked.

My mother came to the door. I could see her breathing. Her face came only to my chest. She was a small, small woman. Ned and I came out of her body. She was my mother.

She stood looking at me through the screen door.

She said, "We knew you got out because our letter came back stamped 'Inmate Released.' "

In the living room, where we all used to live, every bit of it before now, we stood together.

"This is Teddianne," I said. "She's from Cuba. She's my friend."

My mother said, "Well, where are your things? How on earth did you get here? Did you ride the bus up?"

Then I noticed that the house smelled like something; the people there in it, and me, my own past.

I heard Teddianne: "We parked the car down the hill and walked up just now. It's just down on the dirt part of the road. There were nice little flowers all along the way up your hill, in the grass. Little yellow ones," she said.

My mother said, "Daddy's upstairs in Mama K's room. He'll be glad, he'll be real glad."

When I saw my father, he touched me, on the chest, with one hand. He reached out and touched me where he saw. He started to touch Teddianne, but stopped after a little jerk, to do it. I'd seen him do that to people before when he met them, just touch them lightly, or jerk back from it.

He lived a life in this house, in this town.

"Billy-boy. Oh, Billy-Billy," my father said to me, and then saw that she was the one who had been with me even back when I lived in my room in a tent. He knew I had had her then, and in my pocket and my dreams, that this was her.

I should have introduced her to them that way. I should have said, "This is her."

I felt aware of the sun. I looked out the window to it. It

was brighter here. It was pushing something at me. I looked up at it.

"Don't stare at it too long, son. You'll go blind."

"I guess we're just here to be here," I said.

"Might as well stand in the backyard and look up at the moon for all you'll see here in this town," my father said.

"I like it so far," Teddianne said.

He kept looking older and older, and he rubbed his forehead while he did. There were lines there for the years he had spent, living.

"There's a Jesus cloud above this town," I said.

"I don't know, Billy-Billy," my father said. "I don't know about that. I keep thinking, Billy-Billy, whenever I see you, you never should have gotten in that icebox, boy. You were the oldest. You should've known."

Teddianne stood with me in her little space.

I could smell him not knowing, feel him so uneasy, how he'd lived with it too.

Billy-Billy went over to the window and leaned his hands on the sill. He was looking out. I saw his back and how his hair had grown in back. I watched him breathe. I felt something. I turned to see his daddy's face. I followed him down the ancient hallway.

"Sir," I called him. "You shouldn't have said those things about Billy-Billy, to him. He loves Ned. He always talks about him to me.

"He is Ned. He's got both of them in him. It's Ned that keeps Billy-Billy like a child."

"This is a quiet home," Billy-Billy's father said.

I felt like jumping to make a big noise and shake the house, the street, and the town. I looked for Jesus' white hand—maybe it was there, but it was silent. I breathed in for a minute. I stood and looked for His hand.

It was pretty as it went into me.

"I'll go tell Billy-Billy," I thought, "and we'll go out and have a ride in the blue car."

We drove the car off the dirt road; it was red clay. The flowers were there alongside it. I imagined my hand out the window scooping them out of their ground as we drove along. I put my head out the window on my arm and let the wind blow in my face.

We were driving in the downtown, cutting our way out toward the country where Suzanne and her family lived. We drove Eddie's car.

Billy-Billy said, "There's stuff we have to do, with people."

He looked at me. I knew. I didn't care. I cared, but it didn't hurt me, or take me away from him.

"I've known her a long time, but not at all, compared to you."

"It's okay," I told him.

"You look like a church," he said. "Teddianne. I like how your hands are."

He liked to put his finger in the crook of my arm.

I said, "What were those maps in your room, Billy-Billy?"

"I made them out of salt, and flour, and water, and I painted on them," Billy-Billy said.

"They looked red and scary to me," I said.

We rode along; we stopped at a light, people crossing the street in front of the car, some looking in. Billy-Billy hung his arm out the window. He said, "Did you ever have that kind of soap when you were little that when you rubbed away enough, when you washed with it enough, there was a toy inside? I got a toy out of one, once."

"Billy-Billy," I said, "let's drive in a cross. Let's keep driving straight, a long ways, through Mississippi, then Louisiana, Texas, and then go on to New Mexico or somewhere, where it's flat and brown. Then we turn right, and then after a hundred miles, turn around and come back two hundred miles, and then stop, and get out and lie down in the desert, wherever we are, and know we made a cross, a thousand-mile cross. He would see from up above."

"Teddianne," Billy-Billy said, but he didn't say anything more about the cross. He pulled over and pulled me up close to him and held me in the middle of the car seat. I didn't mind him not answering about the cross because I was starting to feel crazy-gone, anyway.

Billy-Billy had that narrow sort of tired look on his face. I felt myself reaching out, spreading out of the car and the town and the world, just spreading up high, so high I could see a thousand-mile cross, easy.

I thought about that, liking it so.

THE
BATHROOM

The sun was shining on something. First, I just enjoyed
the light, then, inside the light, was a place, familiar, swinging. It was the old tire swing from my front yard. I was on
it, high up, then I saw faces. My father's, and Sandy's, my
mother's.

There was a rope coming out of the ground in the middle
of a field. There were woods on either side and the rope
coming up was stringing through a line of people, strung right
through their middles, through their bodies, with holes in
their bodies. I was first, and holding the rope as it came
through, and Billy-Billy was there, farther down the line,
calling to me. There were other people.

"Teddianne," I heard, "Teddianne." The words were
silver.

I felt a hand touching my face.

"It's building," Billy-Billy was saying to me, "the forces,
the nature—"

The shapes were cut out of a darkness, all of us running
around looking for a place to get in.

I saw Billy-Billy's hands shaking on the white cup of

coffee. When the dream was over, we went to a café. I was no angel, but Billy-Billy treated me like one. We ate there. My stomach hurt, so I drank a pitcher of water to make it go away. Then in the bathroom, I leaned my head against the wooded door, to pray. I wanted to pray for Billy-Billy, that nothing bad would happen. I begged Him, to please keep him safe, and with me, that I felt changes coming down here. I stopped praying and just leaned there for a while.

"Holy Mother," I said, "Mother of God." She was once like me, I thought, at least female. "Holy Mary." I didn't want to grow up anymore. I wanted to grow down, back to where I came from.

She spoke to me, two holy words, and they refreshed. I'd tell them to Billy-Billy; I'd keep them inside me for him.

Billy-Billy waited for me at the glass pay counter. I thought of being back in the bathroom against the wooden door, and I imagined I had not just prayed for Billy-Billy but had held myself, too. Had touched myself like Billy-Billy had, inside me. I thought about this, and about what She spoke to me. I should have written things all over the bathroom walls—words about me and Billy-Billy, our secrets, and our names, how they were the same, and how we were always together and could look up in the daytime and see the stars, and how last night he held me and was in me—and how we were buried together somewhere in a big hole.

It was a good morning now. When we got in the car Billy-Billy looked through the windshield with me and said, "We all proceed along paths we create for ourselves."

"Who said that?" I asked.

"Robert E. Lee," Billy-Billy said.

"He didn't," I said.

"You're right," said Billy-Billy, "he didn't."

Billy-Billy drove the car straight out of town onto a quiet road, straight toward the morning sun. We headed toward its huge yellowness, and through it, purified and scarred by it, too. It left a permanent impression of Billy-Billy and me together inside, on our souls where only the deepest scars remain.

Billy-Billy said he was driving slow so we could have time. He said he was nervous about meeting Suzanne. I thought I heard her on the radio. Billy-Billy said no. Then I thought I heard my dad on the same station. Billy-Billy didn't think so.

We were on a dusty road when Billy-Billy said he saw Suzanne. It was the woman who came running out of a house, the front door swinging wide. I saw her bolt out the door with her hair wild behind her, all over, and with a dress on, flying. Her blouse was undone and flapping wide, too. We weren't up to the house yet, and we were moving slow.

Billy-Billy stopped the car. I could see her plainly. She was older than me; she was a woman. She took her shirt and closed it with one hand. She headed straight away from the house, sideways and into a field.

Billy-Billy said she was headed out toward the corn.

I didn't know why things always had to be so dramatic and why we couldn't just visit these people in this town, and in the parlor, and sit and talk. I'd watch and take it all in. I'd be like a glass of milk in their houses. I just wanted to sit in a chair and be here, but this town wouldn't let me. It was so scarred up and marked as any of us.

Billy-Billy parked the car and got out. He stood and watched where she had gone to and then he headed toward the house—where an idiot stood, wearing a helmet, a wild-colored shirt flapping out, and holding a long pole with a whittled, pointed end on it. A spear. Once, Billy-Billy said, Suzanne's parents sent him a Christmas card when he was in the prison, in the summertime, an old one. Like they'd saved it for him, special.

"It's her brother. That's her brother, Lee," Billy-Billy said.

"He's a big one," I said.

The steps were old, and gray wooden. They bowed down where they'd been used. The screen door was wide open, letting the sun and air come in, where she'd run out of. It was an old, white farmhouse sitting alone on a dusty road.

Billy-Billy yelled, "Are you home? Is anyone there?"

Suzanne's brother looked out to the fields and held tight to the stick in his hands. He didn't even look at Billy-Billy or me. He stepped out of Billy-Billy's way is all. A voice came down a narrow-sounding stairwell. It fell down to us.

"Is that you, Billy-Billy Jump? Are you here?"

A woman came clumping down. She came up fast to Billy-Billy.

"Billy-Billy, I didn't know you was home, didn't have any idea," the woman said. "Suzanne, she's . . . did you see her outside? She got out . . . she just runs out."

Billy-Billy looked sick. He stared at the woman.

I could see she was tight as hell, and worn through.

"Who's that?" she asked. She pointed at me.

"She's with me," Billy-Billy said. "She's a friend."

She and Billy-Billy talked about a few things. I stopped

listening at times, wondering what that Suzanne was doing right at that moment and wondering why they weren't wondering, or caring, but I saw how Billy-Billy was wringing his hands, and how his wrists were tight and red.

"It was just unbelievable," said her voice.

I didn't know what, but I looked out and saw Lee on the porch, picking at himself, and leaning his weight around on the old wooden porch. I didn't think it was that unbelievable at all. I was sinking down into my shoes, getting invisible.

"We keep her in her room mostly, wondering what else to do. She draws on the walls, and she cries. We just don't know what to do."

Me and Billy-Billy went up to her room. The mother made coffee and was drinking it alone. I was sweating on my forehead and under my arms—it was dripping down my sides.

I said, "Let's go home, Billy-Billy. I'm feeling scared. We could go home to Secret Town, and be together."

I saw the empty houses in Billy-Billy's eyes and that long, lonely road and the big brown fields to stand in.

There was blood in her bed. The whole room slanted to me then. On the floor was a doll. It had no face. It lay on its front side, but I could tell. It was buckled up, too. The whole thing was bad.

Billy-Billy was looking at a piece of red crepe paper stuck to the ceiling.

Her window had a big X in two boards nailed up on the outside. Billy-Billy went over and kneeled down on the floor to look out through it.

"Billy-Billy," I said. "Oh, Billy-Billy."

"This isn't her life," he said.

"I guess it's all gone," I said.

"You stay here. Then we can go."

"In this room? Want me to stay up here, alone?"

"You could wait outside, or with her mother."

I watched Billy-Billy go down the stairs. I sat down outside on the steps. I felt the day-warm breeze blow on me. I put my knees up close, and rested my head on my hands there. I could see Billy-Billy getting smaller—like a small man, then a boy. Then he was gone.

After he was in the fields for a while, I started to get uneasy. That Lee was outside with me. He caught the same breezes as I did, though; it blew around his big body. It blew in his wild hair, and maybe once he looked at me. Suzanne's mother was inside in the darkness.

I went back up to her room, and closed the door. It looked like it used to be a good room. Now it was like the insides of her. I got down on my knees at the window and saw what I could.

There were some birds in their blue air. The corn was grown tall. Words ran through my head while I watched. I thought I could see right where they were in the corn. The field looked to me like some big, knowing thing. It held them and it could feel them.

I stood near her bed. I pulled the covers over her bloody spot, and kneeled on the bed. I put my head down on her pillow, still on my knees. I wanted to pull back the covers and see the blood. The words went loud in my heart.

I stopped them; pulled down the covers and laid my front side in the spot. It was big, as big as my whole stomach. It wasn't completely dry. I moved my body side to side. I had to. I moved up and down on my stomach, then I was still.

"Billy-Billy!" I heard the screaming. "Billy-Billy! Billy-Billy! . . ." I heard my own voice louder than it had ever been before.

THE FIELDS

I left Teddianne. It was a warm day, and she sat small and quiet on a porch, waiting for me. Suzanne was out, inside a cornfield, crazy in two, and I was going to see her. I thought of her picture that had been on the wall of my cell. Her face, her hair, how her eyes were, looking out.

I'd touched it, worn it down in that cell. I went out to her in the field. I felt Teddianne watching me go. I looked back at her. She got smaller; she didn't wave. I followed where I felt Suzanne was. She'd run into the fields, into a wide space in the corn.

"Suzanne," I said. "Where are you? It's me."

"Here. I'm here."

When I heard her voice, I saw her, piled, curled up in a circle, like a dog, on the ground. She had on old, soft clothes.

When I got closer she opened her eyes to me. She was lying in the black dirt, in a widened, flat-out area in the corn. The stalks were surrounding her. They were thin, parched yellow-green.

I got very close. I squatted down by her. It was her—
it was so her. I saw her eyes.

"Hold me close," she cried. I moved up. I put my arms
around her neck. Her face lay on my shoulder. She said
something to me.

I felt the sweat and the dirt in my eyes. They were wet.
I felt a panic in me, about her.

That's when I heard, like a bird, a tiny voice. "Billy-
Billy! Billy-Billy!" I heard it with my heart. I knew what it
was. I held Suzanne tight to me, crushing her close. She was
warm.

I put one arm behind her neck—it was so thin, the
bones. I reached down underneath her. She let me. I picked
her up. She weighed more than Teddianne.

I carried her out of the fields. I turned and headed for
the house in the distance. Lee was on the porch, alone,
waiting.

"Billy-Billy," she said, "Billy-Billy." She put her mouth,
her whole face, to my neck. "Help me, Billy-Billy."

"I want to. I'm taking you to the house."

She was weak, she felt weak, she was fading. I saw a
face then at the window. It watched me carrying.

Suzanne's mother came outside. Her hands stuck out at
us. We were all out there in the front yard, damned, just
damned.

I saw Teddianne come out onto the porch. Then we were
all out there. We looked at her, at Teddi. She wore a whitish-
colored dress; she wore brown shoes that tied up, with socks
on. On the front of her dress, about the size of a smeared
basketball, was a red stain of blood. Out there in the sunshine
that then seemed to falter and strain some, all of us now in

the yard, and her on the porch, our heads turning, and with a little day breeze—she didn't look out of place.

"Hey, Teddi," I yelled. "You all right?"

"Who's she?" asked Suzanne.

I said, "Teddianne, this is Suzanne. Suzanne—Teddi. She's my friend, from where I'm living now."

"Living?" Suzanne said.

"Yeah. Down in Cuba. It's a long story. It's where I live." Suzanne, standing, now seemed to fall inside herself. We stood in a jagged line, Lee and the mother outside of it. Teddianne on the porch. Suzanne by the steps; they faced me. I felt a weight on me, of time, of a long, long trip. I wavered, and the sun beat down, burning on to us the scars. We live and live, over and over, and keep on doing it, slow and slow. It got like a heavy weight.

"I want to go in now, Mama," said Suzanne. She was almost back to the ground. "I have to rest," she said. "I want y'all to come back, though, come back out here after dark."

We stared, and our eyes drooped down.

"Teddianne—you come, Teddianne. I like your name. I know you, like a toy, like a pretty ray. Will you come?"

Teddianne said, "I guess so. I guess I know we will."

"We'll be back, after dark," I said. "There'll be a moon, and we'll be back." The wild side, I thought, the wild side will be out.

"This farm," I said. "It's changing, it's like a disc-thing, like a slow-turning thing, like it's on a wheel from down below it." I knew it was shifting, trying to change time.

"We gotta go," I said. "Then Teddianne and me will be back."

We walked to the blue car.

"What's he looking at?" I asked.

Lee was staring at nothing, in the air, as if in every direction at once.

"He's looking for the devil, I guess," said Suzanne. And she said to me, "So do the devil a favor, will you, when you come back, and get her a Pepsi?"

THE WILD BLUE CAR

We drove fast through the dust back to town. Teddianne changed her clothes in the car. "A Pepsi," she said. "I can't believe it." She pulled her dress over her head. She tugged at it. Her stomach was crowding her tattoo.

She threw her dress out the window, and rode with the sun and the air on her.

She reached in back, then she climbed over. She got into her shirt and pants. We watched each other in the rear-view mirror.

"Watch the road, boy! Don't hit nothing."

"I like that dress you threw out the window. I liked that dress more than I like my parents. It just blew away. Even with that red on it."

We drove and we slid and threw up dust, and it was funny. There was a flock of small birds beating their wings like crazy up ahead going through the blue sky, keeping ahead of us in their little lives.

I drove fast.

• • •

Billy-Billy drove too fast. I watched him, and the ground going by. I tried to focus on one small thing while the rest blurred by. It was hard; I felt so small in the car. We were both laughing, and flying, and then not laughing, too. We flew in the car. I screwed my neck out the window, hoping to see a big star, pointing the way, but there wasn't any, not in the daytime.

In my mind I kept a small secret. I prayed, I wished, I closed my eyes while Billy-Billy flew along. I asked Jesus to come down tonight and heal us all of what we needed healed.

"Please," I prayed, "show Yourself to me, again." I prayed and I rocked myself back and forth in the wild blue car. I visualized His face in my heart, and saw It. I looked at It, and held on to It, in Its wonder.

When I opened my eyes, I saw Billy-Billy, all turned around, watching me.

"Geez, watch the road—" We were running through a red light, and other cars were honking. It wasn't a big town. We kept going.

Billy-Billy said, "Got any more dresses to throw out, baby? Throw them out now, on Main Street. . . . Whahoo! Billy-Billy Jump's back in town."

He drove straight to his own street. He drove the car past his house with a roar and a flash of blue. Oh, Eddie, it was good he didn't come along. Billy-Billy rolled down the dirt road. I just barely saw the spot where we slept the night before.

He pulled up a narrow lane. We were in a cemetery. Billy-Billy drove the car onto the grass. He drove over the graves, and spun the car in circles, tearing up the grass and the dirt. All those people were stretched out, lying underneath us in the ground. I saw them in their best clothes, laid out and long.

I screamed from the backseat. I didn't know what else to do.

"This is bad, Billy-Billy! Stop it! This is bad!"

"Look," Billy-Billy yelled. "There's Ned."

Billy-Billy stopped and got out. I got out, too. I held my arm around him. He was shaking. He didn't know what was happening. He held himself at a wild angle. The whole place looked like it was involved, that it was a wild thing, too.

He put his open hands on top of the grave. The stone read his name, Ned Jump. I saw he died in 1953. We sat down near the grave and touched our hands together.

We had a calm for a while. There were no other people around to see, or to see us. The *seeing*, I guess, was a thing in itself.

God was staring at us from around behind Ned's gravestone.

We walked through the dead people. We stepped between them, sometimes. Sometimes I walked right on top of them. I let my feet sink in. Teddianne stood and waited for me when I did that.

I didn't go back to my house. I let them be there without me. I never saw my father alive again in this world. I knew we were all in the same sea. I saw his dirt mound in this

very same place, just a throw away from where Teddianne
and I walked and where she was so herself and gave me some
of it to keep.

We read the stones there, and each other. We had one
mind then. I saw: maybe she will come back to me.

We waited out there until our faces turned dark with the early
night. We sat at a tree to our backs. I felt her breathing with
me.

"Is it time yet?" I said.

"Not quite yet," she said.

We waited until it was darker. I couldn't see her face
very well. It was hidden from me, but with the glow I'd known
the first time when she took me to Secret Town Road and left
me at the hillbank.

"Now?" I said. "Now can we go?"

"Yeah," she said. "Yeah, it's good now. We can go."
She got up. And she started to dance.

She danced all around me. She was wild. She was driven.
She was funny, she was having fun. She kept doing it. She
was sweating, and making something. She danced right through
me. Her teeth pointed. Her lips flared back. She kept working, dancing, for me.

She danced and spun the whole thing out into now, when
she jumped up and over to me, and lay down, wet and bright
and out of breath. She seemed to stop breathing for a while,
her head in my lap. Then she took my hand. She walked me
to the blue car. I felt myself tall. I was really tall. I had to
hunch my shoulders to keep from missing the sky.

"A spoon," I said. "There's a spoon in my mind."

TRIANGLE
OF LIGHT

I was driving down the cemetery lane. We passed in front of the Masonic Home. The spinning wheel was still there. We went past my house, where a light was on. I saw Teddianne living there along with us even when I was a child, her sitting with her legs pulled up under her, in shorts, or at the kitchen table eating toast, dripping jelly, and catching it with her tongue, while we all lived around her.

At the road to Suzanne's house, we went over the cross of the two-road intersection. I pulled my feet up off the car floor. We slowed down some and listened to the rolling of the tires.

"There went that boy!" Teddianne shouted. "That Lee, brother guy. Look!"

Sure enough, there he was. "Let's go," I said. "Let's follow Lee."

He came riding his red night-bike right at us, just before the curve would put his back to us. And he was smiling, he wasn't dumb, and he wasn't playing. He was eating up the place, sucking in the air and making it holy. An entire picture was forming, dawning on me, like looking through a tiny hole at another world, and that Lee was the doorway.

I remembered a point, that day as a boy, in the doctor's office, when I'd seen part of it before, the great solved thing. I'd run my whole life, to get from that point to this wide-open place. Now it had a face on it.

"Teddianne!" I yelled. I saw her, moving herself forward to get closer. We were at the outer edge of his place, the gravel, circle path he rode. I wondered if he knew what he was. The house itself sat silent, swollen-looking, squatting down toward the ground. It looked empty, but with a watchfulness inside.

He looped by again. He looked at us in the same way.

I felt like a child. My head in a small circle, with a new haircut on. My innocence was.

I sat in a smoky field, and I tasted someone's blood in my mouth.

Teddianne was a different kind of girl. I saw her back in front of me, like in a haze. Her tattoo, it became a painting that seeped out from inside her. And she was.

"Look at his face!" I yelled to Teddianne. "Look at it!"

He came at us. His face was long, and narrow, baggy-looking, with flat brown hair on the top and sides. His eyes were hung down, full of white. His mouth worked open and closed, showing his teeth, with big gaps between them.

That's where I started to go, to lose track of time.

I heard sniffing noises from Teddianne.

He smiled.

There were other people standing near the circle, watching. Teddianne wept, in her hands.

Someone lay down in the middle grass part of the gravel

area, on their back. It was starting to get scary. I wished we were home, anywhere. I thought of Eddie, safe at home. I had a dumb thought: "I haven't played any baseball this summer. I haven't done anything good, or fun, for years."

"Teddianne," I yelled to her. "What's happening? I feel crazy here."

"I have to touch him. I have to touch him with my hands," she said. "I have to. I know why we came here. This is where it begins."

There were people everywhere, cut out of the darkness. There was the one man, and now others, rolling in the grass. There was a face at a window.

Teddianne said, she turned and talked over her shoulder at me, "Not just anybody could get here—I have to get closer, to see."

The noise of a car came up fast. I looked down to it and saw Suzanne in the headlights. She was staring out at me and Lee at the same time. Her face was twisted from inside her, like barbed wire. One hand was flattened on her stomach.

I'd stuck out a man's eyes for her.

In the lights, the place was lit. The face at the window watched. He must have been on his knees or bent over low. His hand was holding the bottom of the window shade.

Lee fell over from the bicycle; it tipped over at Teddianne's feet. She reached out and touched him, she helped him to his feet. He got back on and went out toward the fields.

We followed. He rode, parting the tall grass like water. Suzanne came after us, at a distance, holding up her dress in her hand.

"Hope those people don't follow us," Teddianne said. "Who were they, anyway?"

I looked back, toward where they had been; I just saw Suzanne.

"I don't know," I told her.

We got to a little cleared area. Lee turned toward us and with his hand to his mouth, he looked at us, long; he stared. I noticed Suzanne doing the same, her hand was held up, but different; she pressed her mouth. The moonlight shone down on her head.

As we sat, a triangle got made among us, a triangle of light. I could see Lee's and Teddianne's eyes clearly lit by it. Suzanne got lit at her distance. And in that shape, we were.

The light wrapped us and connected.

Suzanne's face got orangy gold from it.

"The light is what I *am*," I knew. A thousand yellow-white suns opened up inside my chest. I saw it rush through Secret Town as a heart-place. It came out of everywhere. It followed after me down all the roads and places I'd been, and inside of Teddianne, and the past all became lit up to the point where we were.

We stayed there like that, for a little while in the night.

ADELE

The sun came up. We stayed in the area for two more days. We saw things. Some people came and went. Everything I saw looked different, like it held something. Some people brought presents and candy, and fruit-flavored drinks. Lee liked only the lemonade. He sat outside and stared at his bicycle.

Teddianne was changed. She was quiet. She wasn't a girl, as young, like she used to be. But she still had her hands up at her face, and in her yellow hair. She stroked her forehead and watched that Lee.

He made drawings, mostly of things I couldn't understand.

Suzanne combed her hair, that had turned red, beautiful.

He pulled Teddianne in his red wagon behind the red bicycle. He pulled her in a worn-out, smooth circle.

I drove the bike one evening. It was nice holding the grips and feeling the twilight air. I wasn't missing anything anywhere in the world. We lingered there then.

He held out something for me to take. It was a large pencil drawing on a big, rolled-up piece of paper. It looked like a map. There was the pattern that made no sense, but it had a power on it, and his style spread all over it.

Teddi said Jesus had come down that one night and had seen us up close.

He said the word to us, his name, directly handed down: "Adele."

We stood there, ready to go, too, starting to forget really why we'd ever come.

Suzanne held Teddianne. They laughed about something, the sound came out like smoke from their mouths.

Suzanne looked like someone's mother, even to the air she walked through and to the grass and brown colors under her feet.

UNTIL TUESDAY

We drove home in the blue car, past all the things we'd seen. Teddianne rode the last part in the backseat. At first we rode together, up front, close; she got the dash light on her face. When we got home we talked to Eddie in the kitchen about the trip. He listened, and then he got mad about the car. He said that today was Tuesday, and that he had to go to the bank to get money to pay the Coke man.

He was cracking around in the kitchen light.

He said, "On account of you, I had to ride with him all the way downtown in a Coca-Cola truck."

AS A CHILD

Teddianne and me; we had the fall together. We saw some of that light around town, it was in us, but we never said much about it.

Teddianne wore new blue jeans that were stiff, and bright; they rubbed together at her legs when she walked, making that sound. She liked it when I got behind her and watched how she looked.

She'd watch me over her shoulder. It was clear and clean then.

And Teddianne was the kind of girl, that if I asked her to wait for me, to be somewhere, then she'd stand there and wait, even in the rain, standing somewhere on a street corner, waiting for me forever.

I noticed that she had only one line running across her palms, each one the same. She said it was that way, new, since she touched that Lee when he fell down from his bicycle. We walked around the block, circles in the neighborhood at night, in the pitch dark.

I watched Teddianne one night, the night Harry's great-granddaughter was born. His granddaughter called Eddie's to tell. Harry had no phone 'cause he couldn't hear a little sound. Teddianne got the message. She went over to tell Harry the news. I leaned my chin on the windowsill; I was on my knees, watching.

She walked across the street-lighted way to Harry's house. I saw her out there tapping on Harry's door. She tapped on his windows. She slid her hands along the house, delicately. She jumped on the grass. She made a quick turn looking up at the house where I was. She made faces at the night.

She banged once more, hard, and Harry blew a bullet through the window into her forehead. Her hand went out behind her, in the shape of a star, held out to break her fall.

AS GOD

Teddianne used to have a scar on her forehead, above her eyebrow, where a boy hit her, as a child, for not loving God. But it was me who said her name, because I'd heard that if you said the name of God over and over again, you would become Him.

BECAUSE
IT WAS
YELLOW

Looking for a ride back out of town, a few days later, hitching, I went down a side street and saw ahead, walking toward me, a little girl, alone. She was zigzagging down the street, wearing a red rain slicker with the hood up. She carried a lunch box in her hand and was swinging it back and forth. It was a quiet scene, just her swinging all alone on this street that curved uphill behind her.

When we got close, I saw her face. She was swinging her head around like the lunch box. I got even with her. I never wanted to get past that point.

I traveled slow, thinking about the big Jesus cross. I kept looking at the map I had.

I spent my first three months alone at a hotel near the shore. It was yellow-painted wood. They let me work there—it was winter and slow—for as little as one hour a day. My room was the smallest one, near the end of another slanted hallway.

In my room were pegs on the wall for coats. Soon, all of my clothes were there, or draped across the chair back. They were the only witnesses to what I did in there. I sat with my eyes closed. I let go, I let myself go out as far as I could.

And I played—on the rug in my room, with toys, cars, and little men. I reduced my world, to the floor, to the corners—it bumped into the thin lattice-board boundaries that I couldn't go past.

I thought of her. I waited. Sometimes, I raised my head to look out the window at the sea.

A NOTE ABOUT THE AUTHOR

Rudy Wilson has a degree from the University of Iowa,
and now makes his home in a small town in Iowa. This
is his first novel.

A   N O T E   O N   T H E   T Y P E

This book was set in a digitized version of Bodoni Book,
named after Giambattista Bodoni (1740–1813), son of a
printer of Piedmont. After gaining experience and fame
as superintendent of the Press of the Propaganda in Rome,
in 1768 Bodoni became the head of the ducal printing
house at Parma, which he soon made the foremost of its
kind in Europe. His *Manuale Tipografico*, completed by
his widow in 1818, contains 279 pages of type specimens,
including alphabets of about thirty languages. His edi-
tions of Greek, Latin, Italian, and French classics are
celebrated for their typography. In type designing he was
an innovator, making his new faces rounder, wider, and
lighter, with greater openness and delicacy, and with
sharper contrast between the thick and thin lines.

Composed by Crane Typesetting Service, Inc.,
Barnstable, Massachusetts
Printed and Bound by The Haddon Craftsmen, Inc.,
Scranton, Pennsylvania

Designed by Julie Duquet